BENNY AND PENNY

IN

THE BIG
NO-NO!

GEOFFREY HAYES

BENNY AND PENNY

IN

THE BIG NO-NO!

A TOON BOOK BY

GEOFFREY HAYES

TOON BOOKS IS A DIVISION OF RAW JUNIOR, LLC, NEW YORK

Spotlight

For Debby Carter

Editorial Director: FRANÇOISE MOULY

Book Design: FRANÇOISE MOULY & JONATHAN BENNETT

GEOFFREY HAYES' artwork was drawn in colored pencil.

ABDOPUBLISHING.COM

Reinforced library bound edition published in 2015 by Spotlight, a division of ABDO
PO Box 398166, Minneapolis, Minnesota 55439. Spotlight produces high-quality reinforced library bound
editions for schools and libraries. Published by agreement with Candlewick Press.

Printed in the United States of America, North Mankato, Minnesota.
112014
012015

THIS BOOK CONTAINS
RECYCLED MATERIALS

LIBRARY OF CONGRESS CATALOGING-IN-PUBLICATION DATA

This book was previously cataloged with the following information:

Hayes, Geoffrey.
Benny and Penny in The big no-no! : a Toon Book / by Geoffrey Hayes.
p. cm.
Summary: Two mice meet their new neighbor and discover that she is not as scary as they feared.
ISBN 978-0-9799238-9-0
1. Graphic novels. [1. Graphic novels. 2. Mice--Fiction. 3. Brothers and sisters--Fiction. 4. Neighbors--
Fiction.]
I. Title. II. Title: Big no-no!
PZ7.7.H39Be 2009
[E]--dc22

2008036307

978-1-61479-300-7 (reinforced library bound edition)

Spotlight

A Division of ABDO
abdopublishing.com

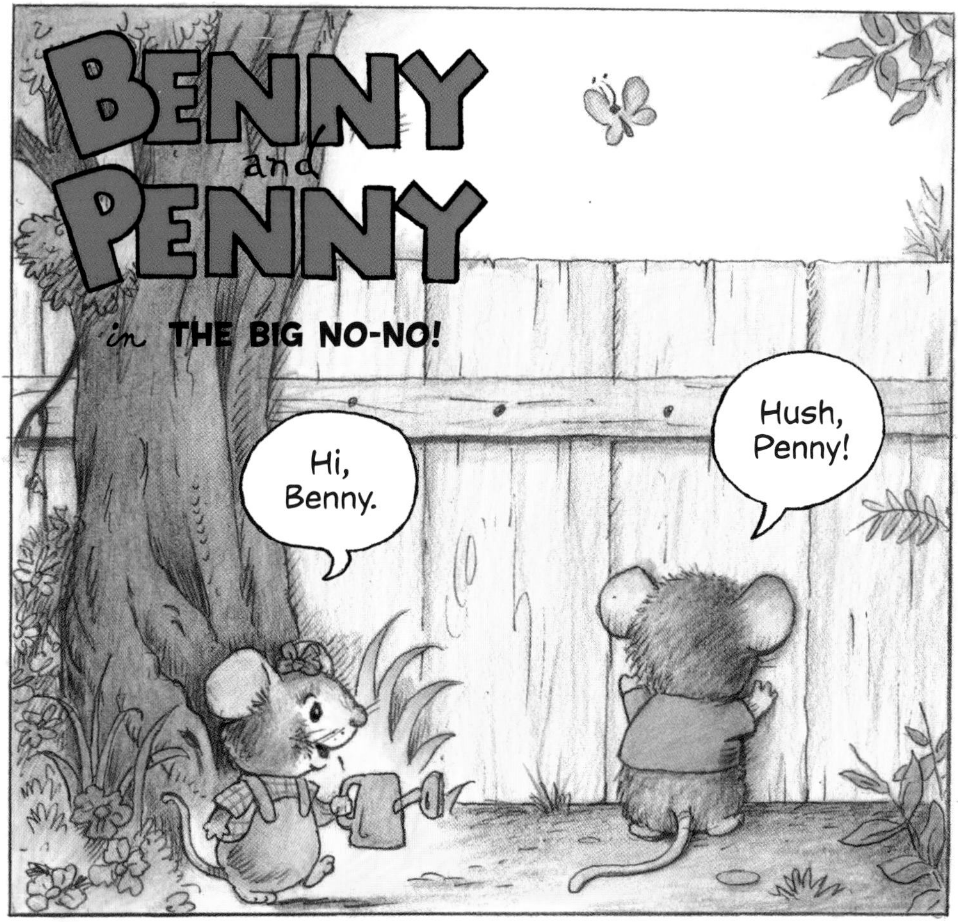
BENNY and PENNY
in THE BIG NO-NO!
Hi, Benny.
Hush, Penny!

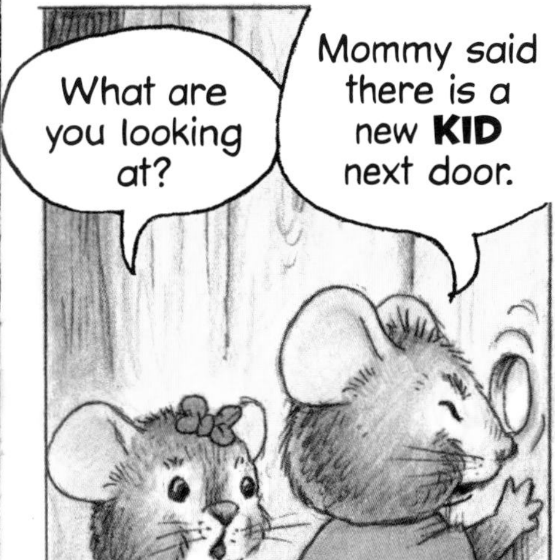
What are you looking at?
Mommy said there is a new **KID** next door.

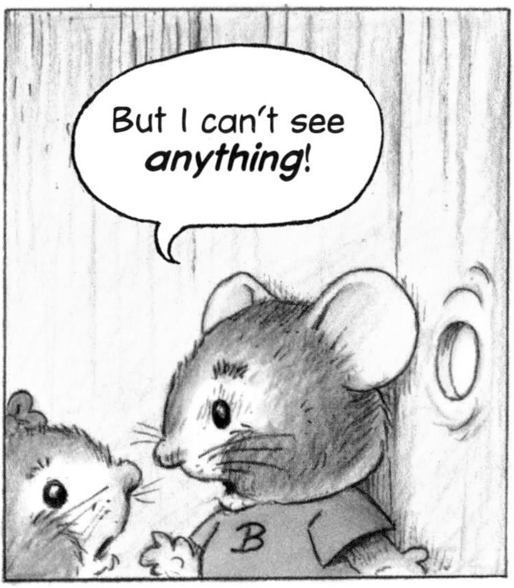
But I can't see ***anything***!

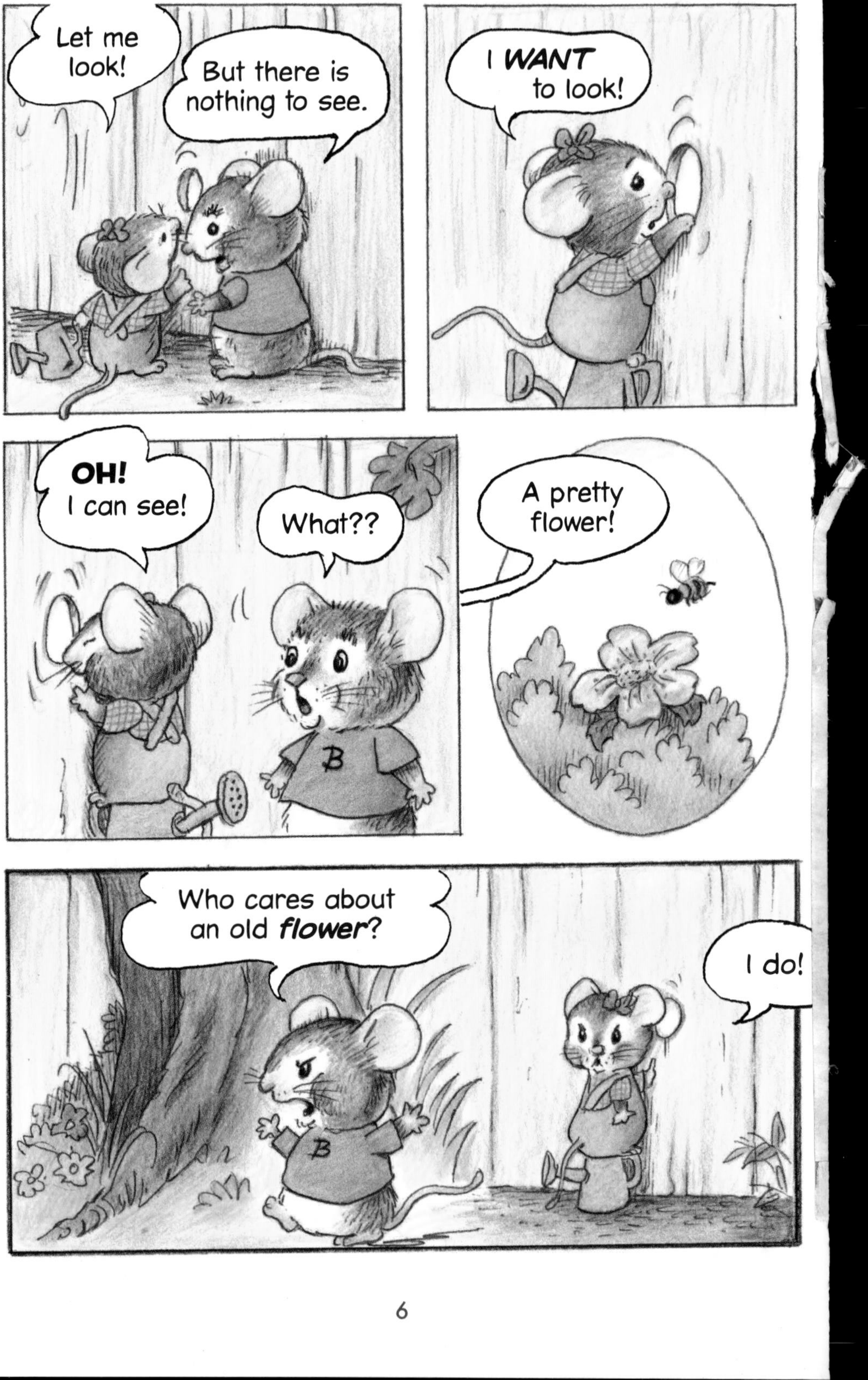
Let me look!
But there is nothing to see.
I WANT to look!
OH! I can see!
What??
A pretty flower!
Who cares about an old flower?
I do!

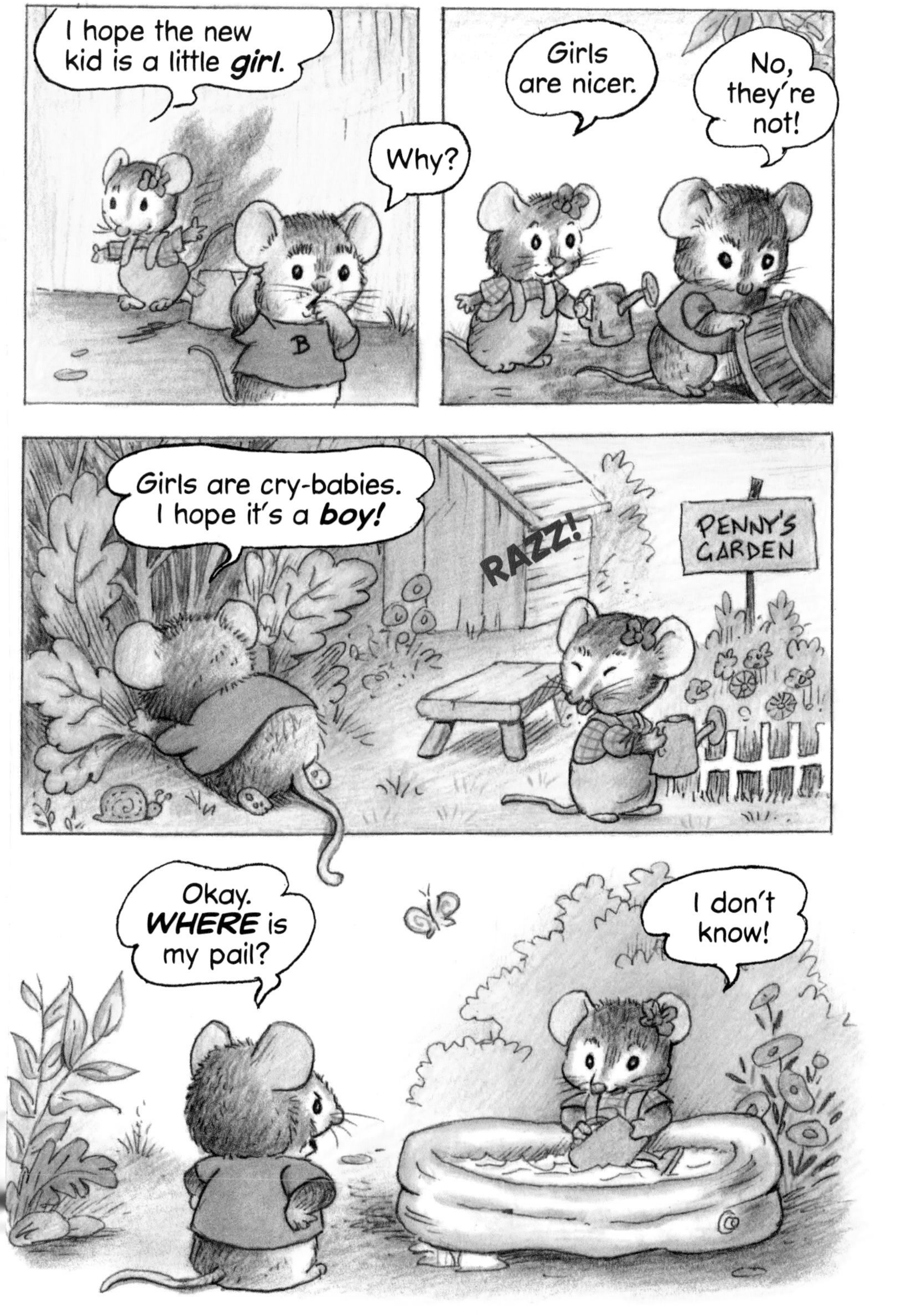
I hope the new kid is a little ***girl***.
Why?
Girls are nicer.
No, they're not!
Girls are cry-babies. I hope it's a ***boy!***
RAZZ!
PENNY'S GARDEN
Okay. ***WHERE*** is my pail?
I don't know!

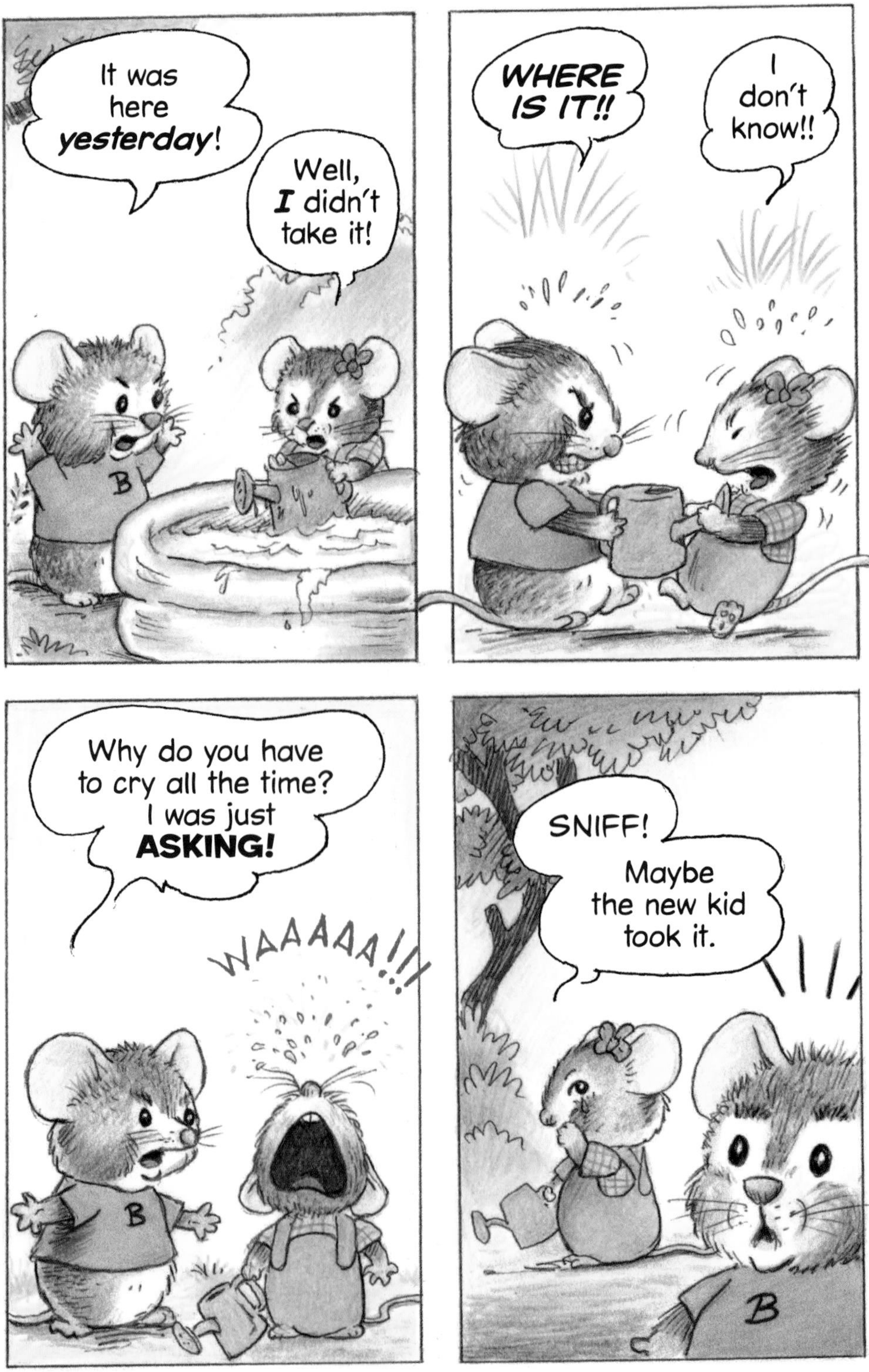
It was here *yesterday*!
Well, *I* didn't take it!
WHERE IS IT!!
I don't know!!
Why do you have to cry all the time? I was just **ASKING!**
WAAAAA!!!
SNIFF!
Maybe the new kid took it.

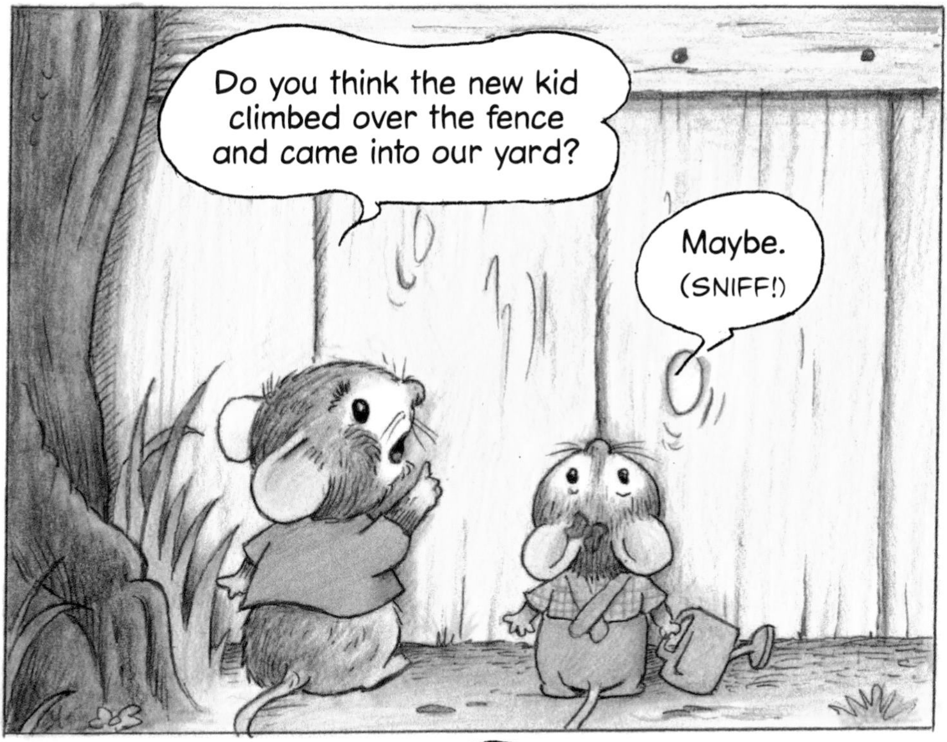

Do you think the new kid climbed over the fence and came into our yard?
Maybe. (SNIFF!)

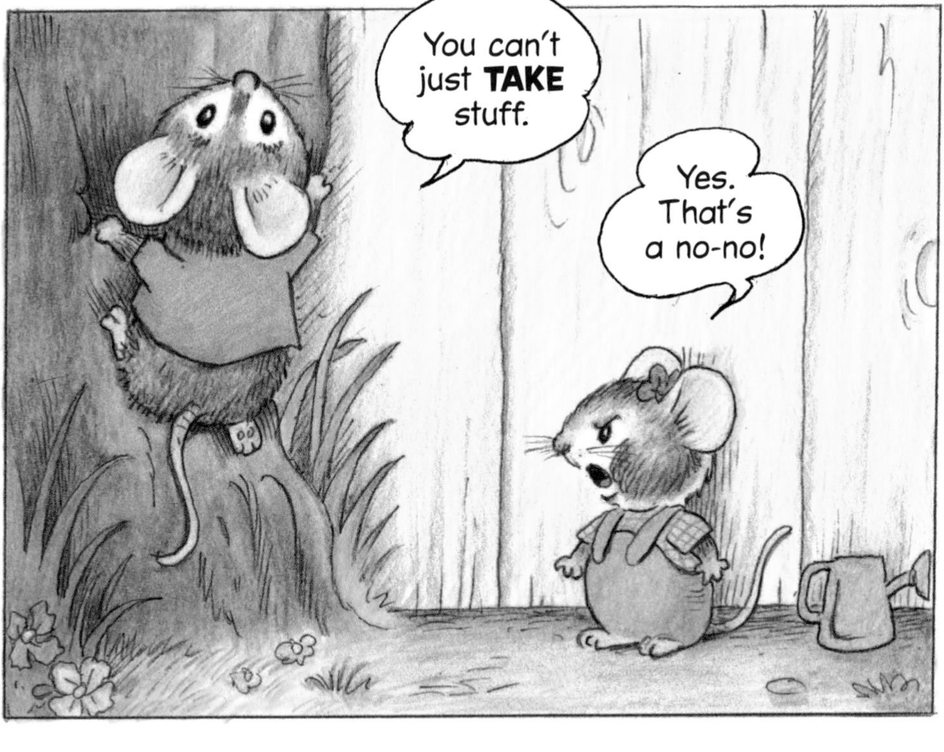

You can't just **TAKE** stuff.
Yes. That's a no-no!

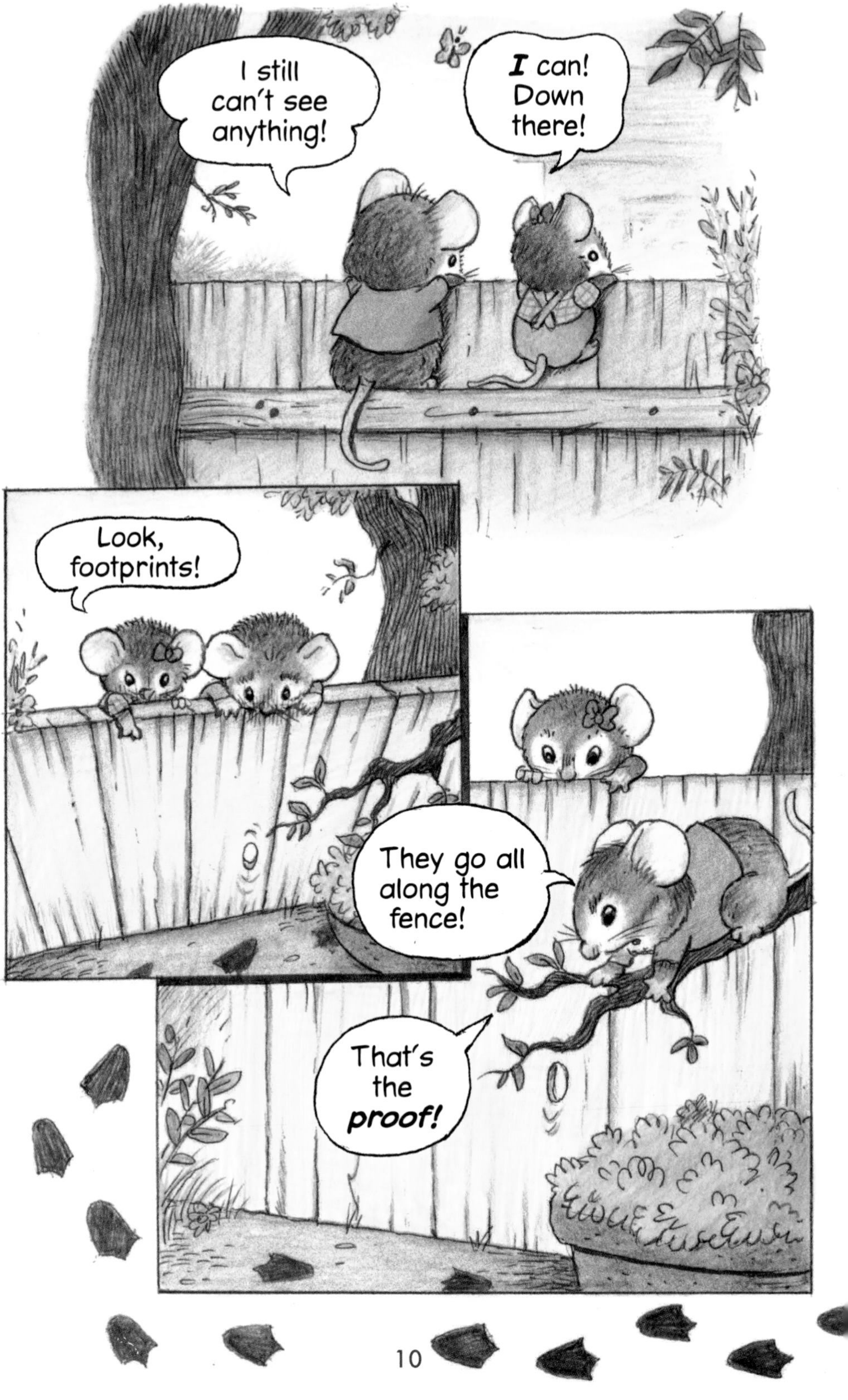
I still can't see anything!
I can! Down there!
Look, footprints!
They go all along the fence!
That's the ***proof!***

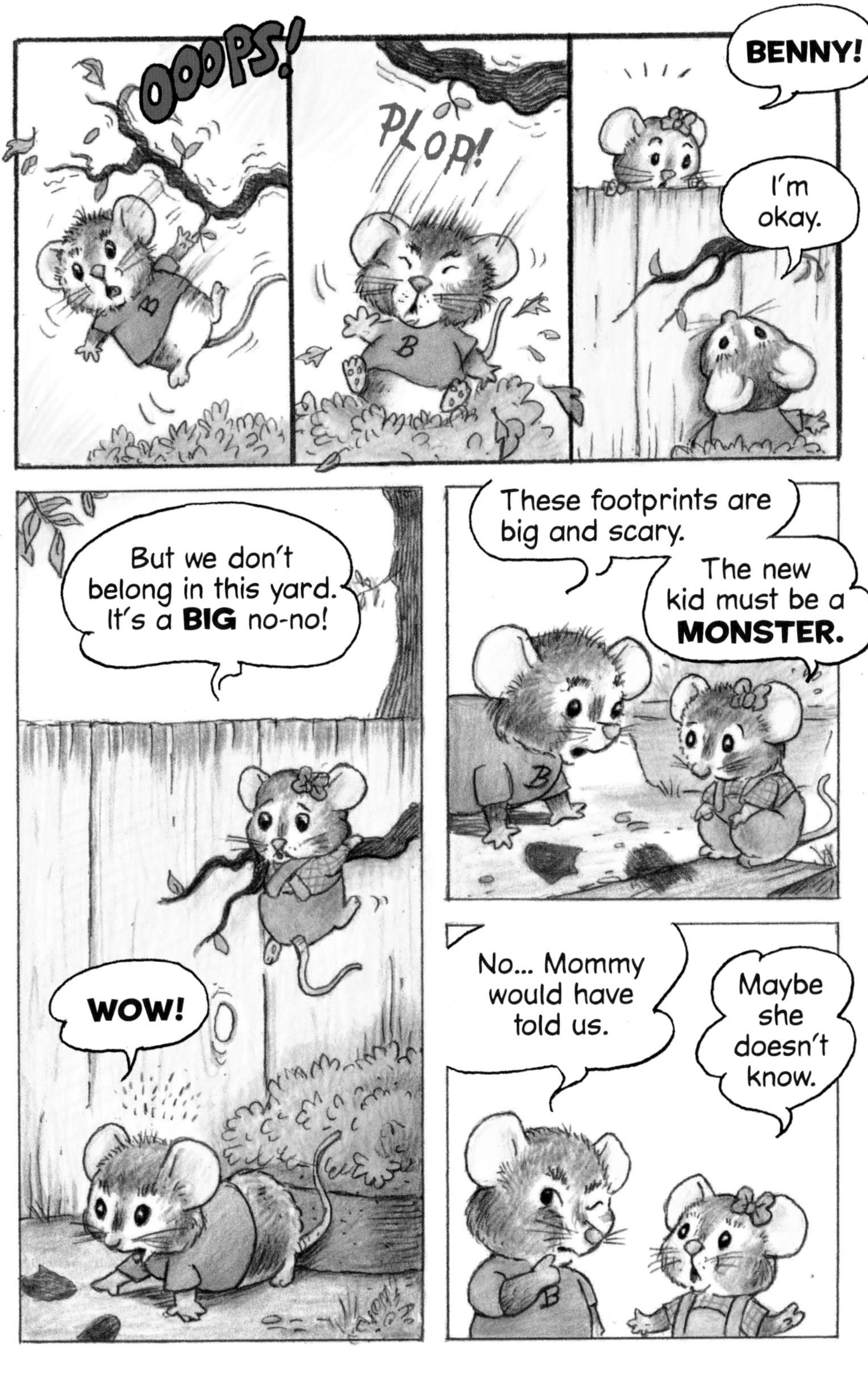
OOOPS!
PLOP!
BENNY!
I'm okay.
But we don't belong in this yard. It's a BIG no-no!
WOW!
These footprints are big and scary.
The new kid must be a MONSTER.
No... Mommy would have told us.
Maybe she doesn't know.

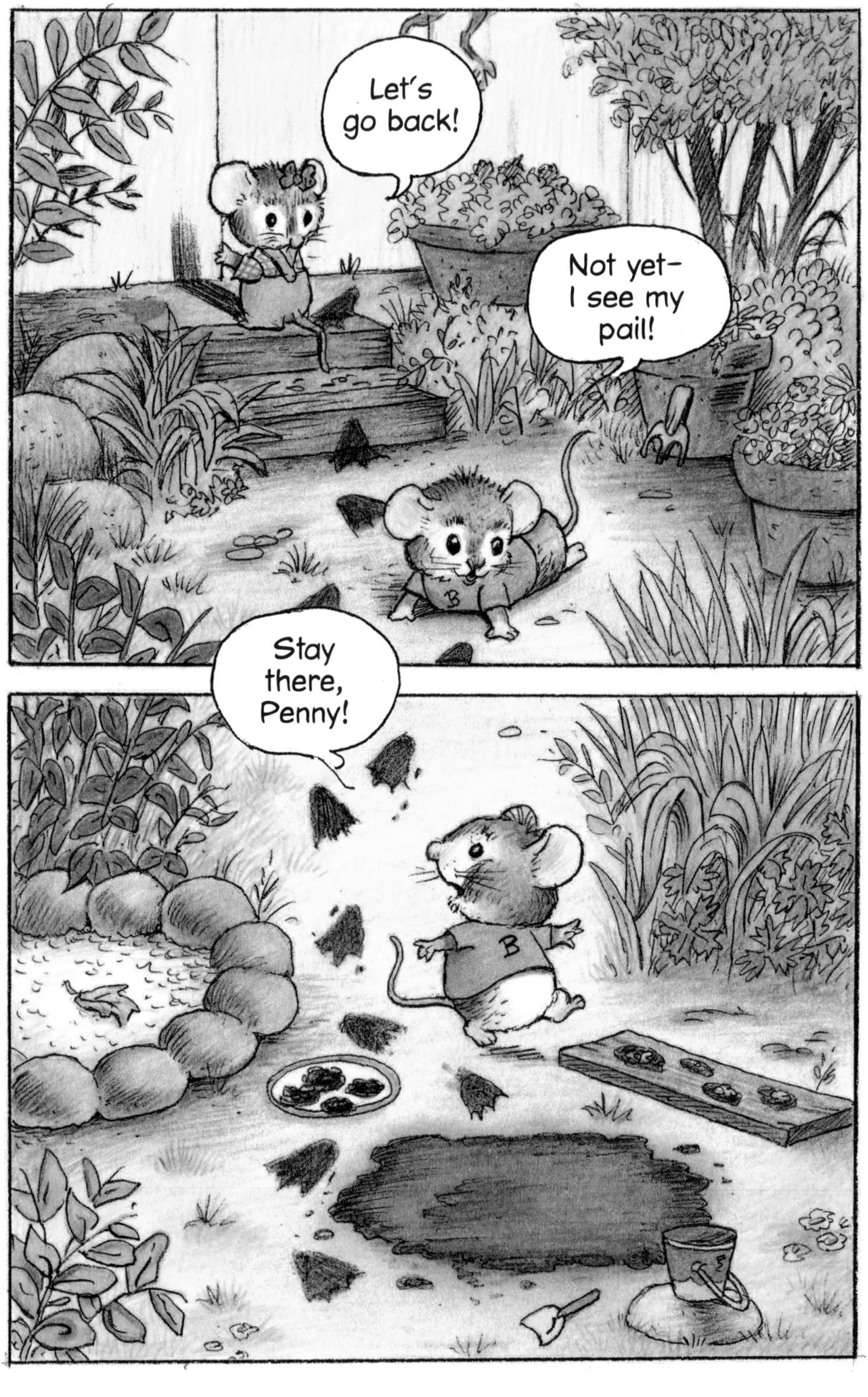
Let's go back!
Not yet- I see my pail!
Stay there, Penny!

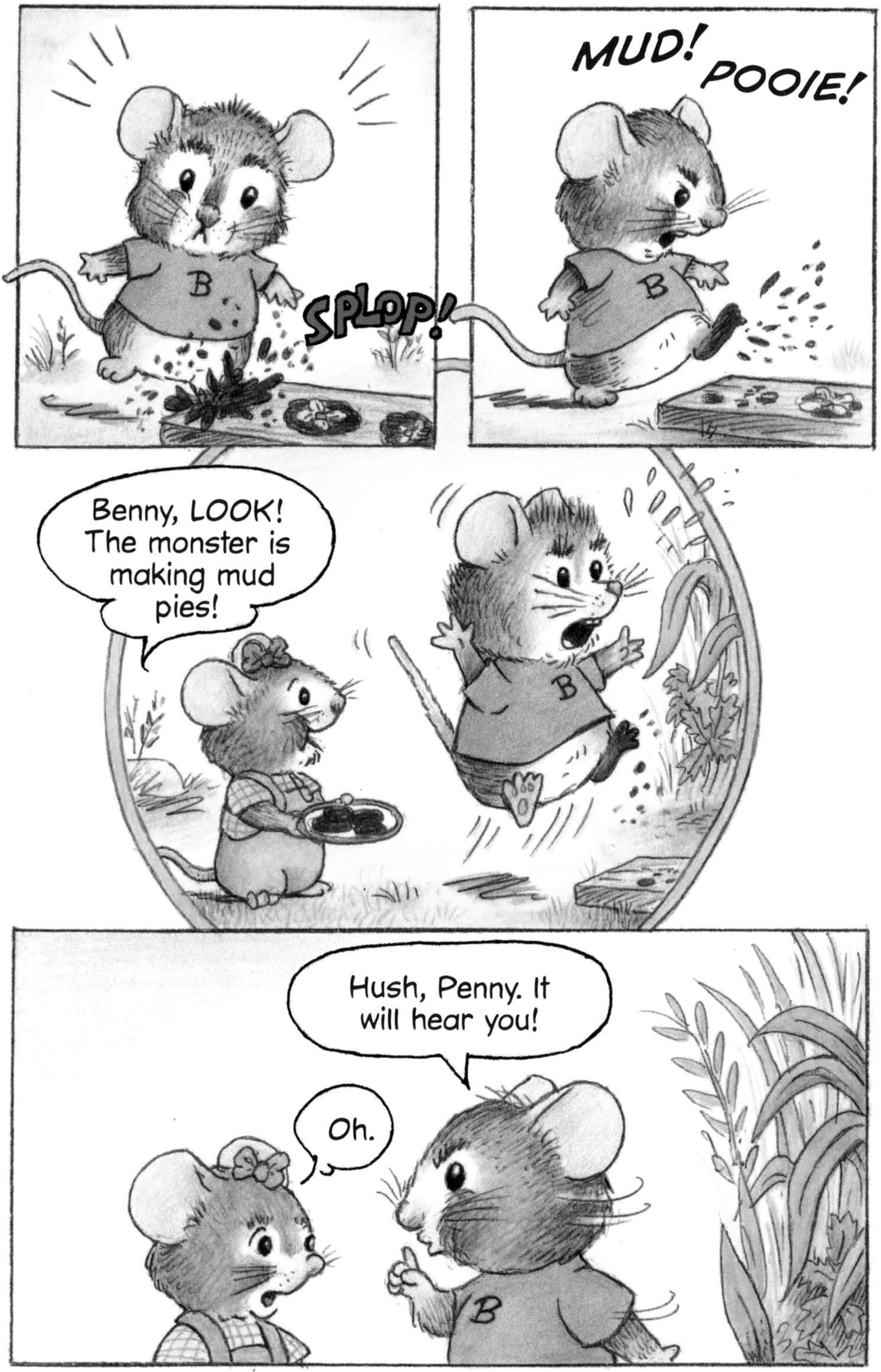
SPLOP!
MUD!
POOIE!
Benny, LOOK! The monster is making mud pies!
Hush, Penny. It will hear you!
Oh.

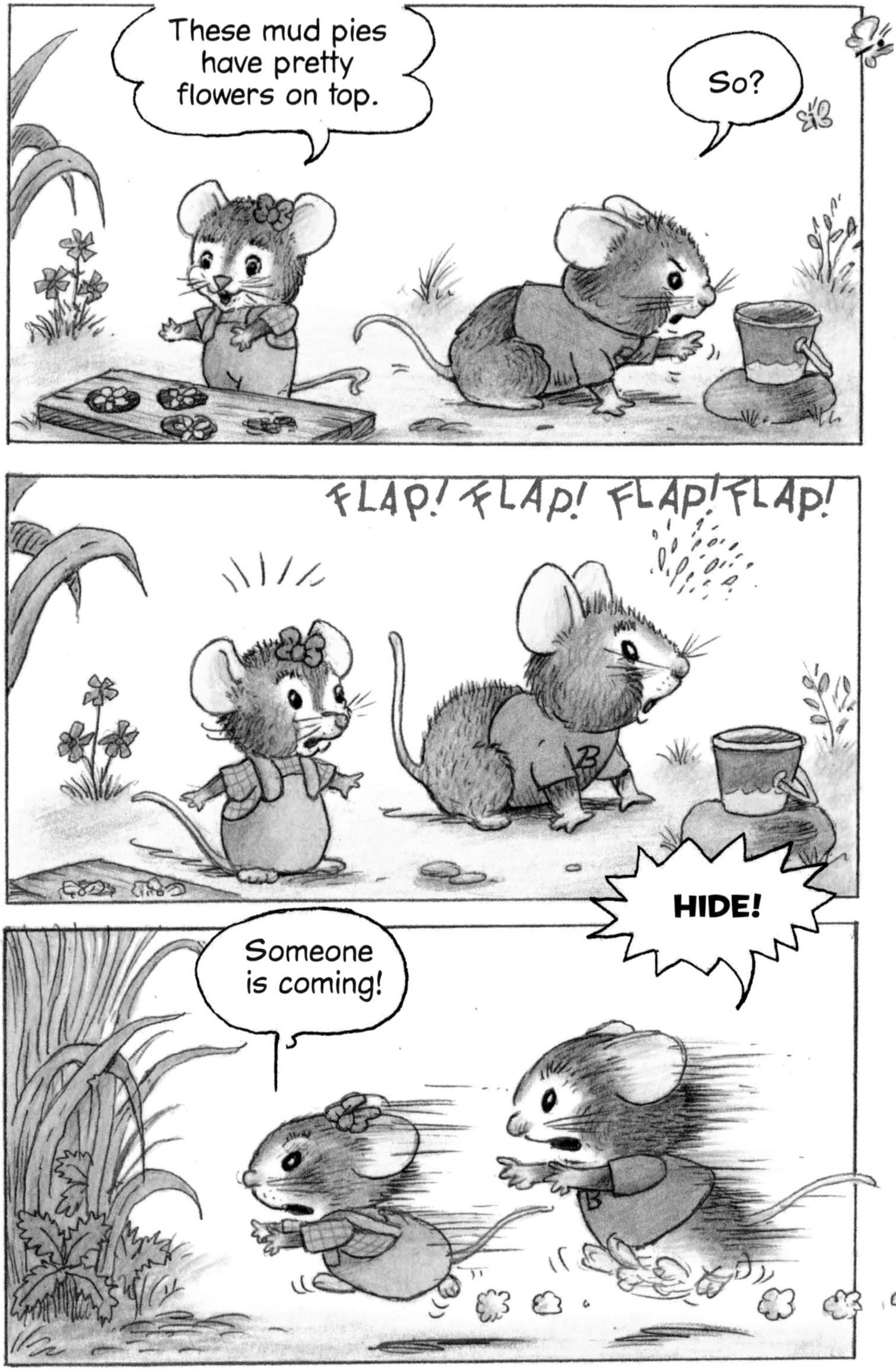
These mud pies have pretty flowers on top.
So?
FLAP! FLAP! FLAP! FLAP!
HIDE!
Someone is coming!

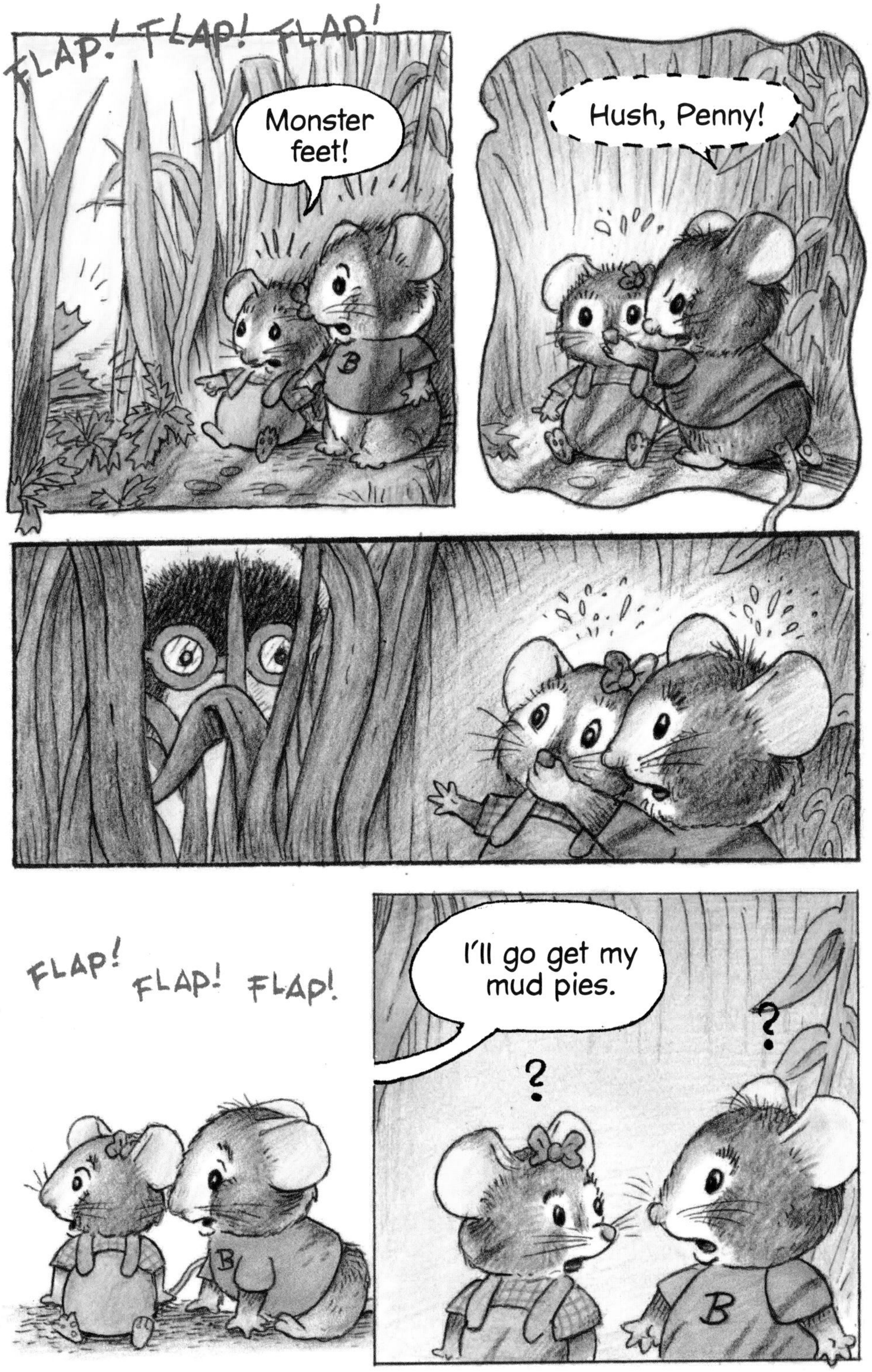
FLAP! FLAP! FLAP!
Monster feet!
Hush, Penny!
FLAP! FLAP! FLAP!
I'll go get my mud pies.
?
?

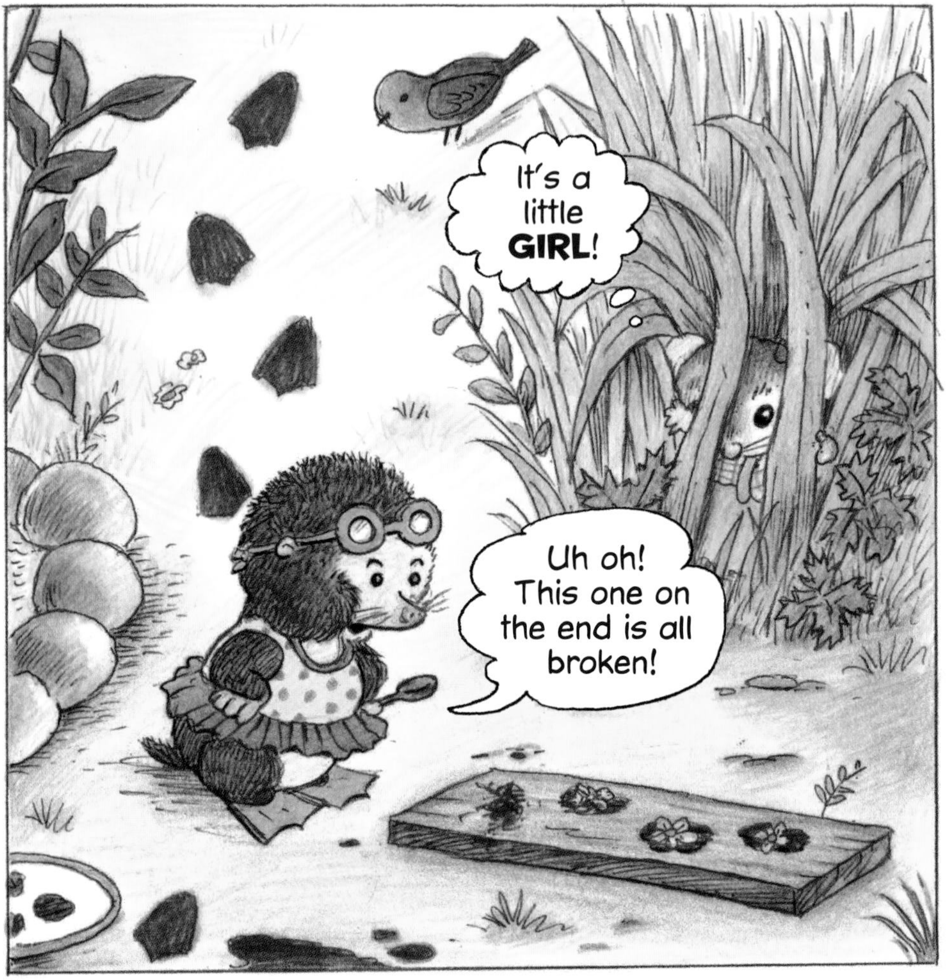
It's a little **GIRL**!
Uh oh! This one on the end is all broken!

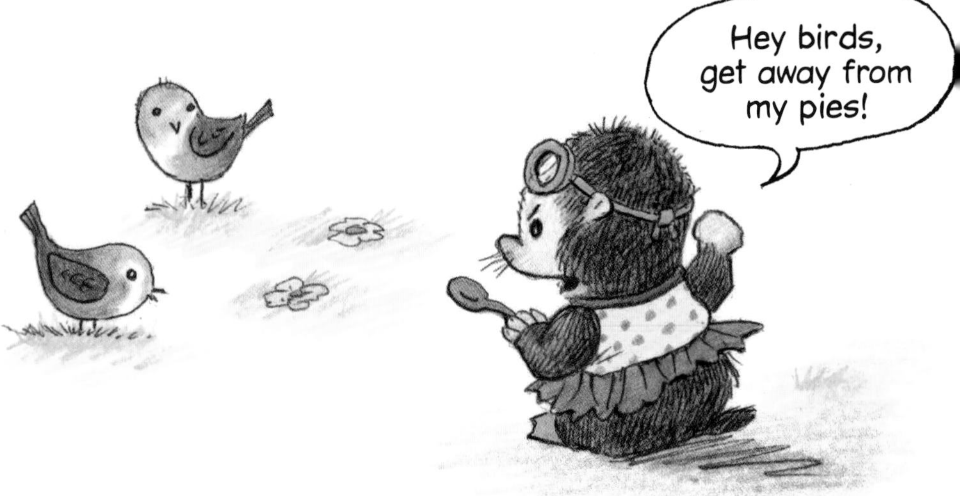
Hey birds, get away from my pies!

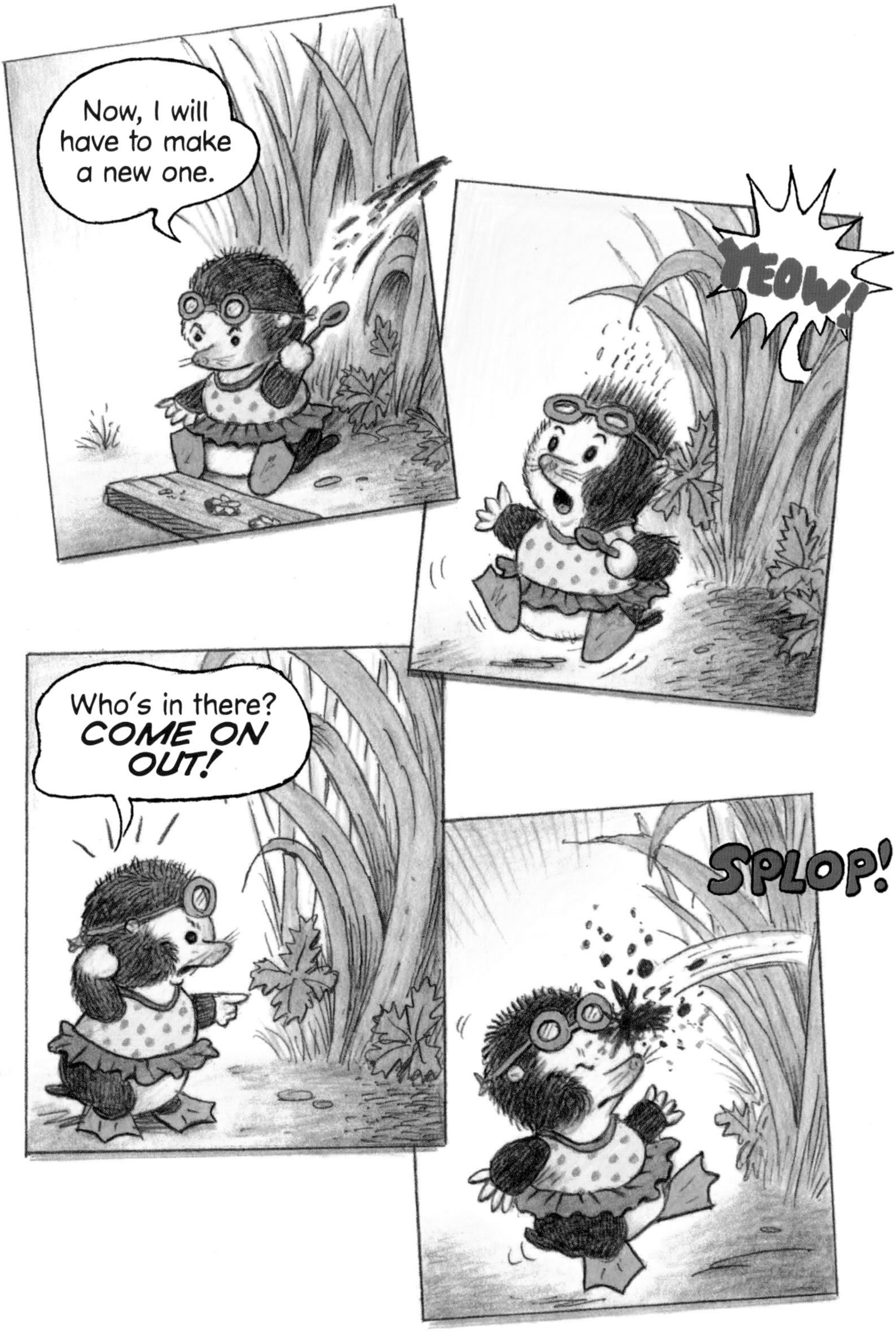
Now, I will have to make a new one.
YEOW!
Who's in there? COME ON OUT!
SPLOP!

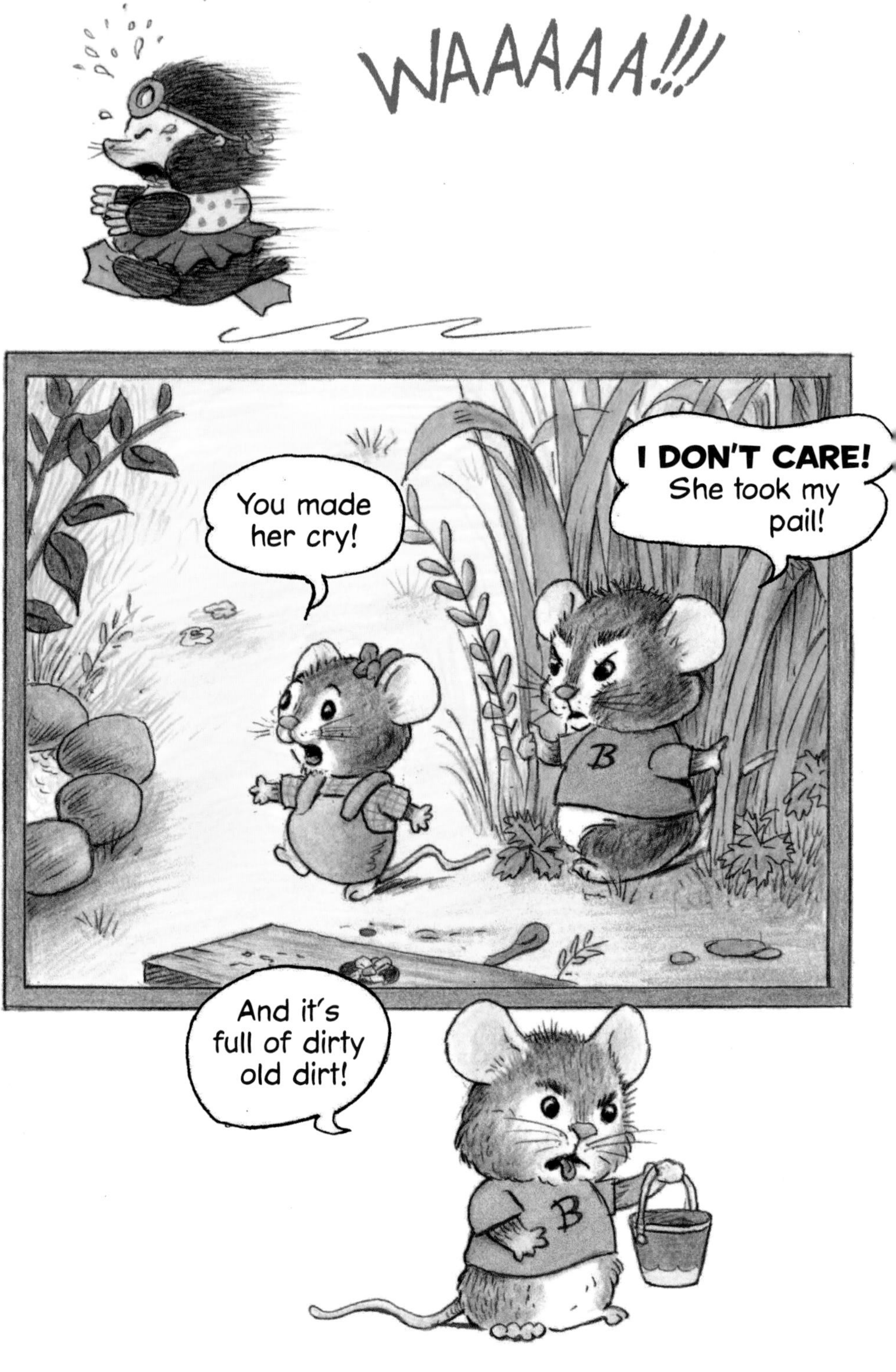
WAAAAA!!!
You made her cry!
I DON'T CARE! She took my pail!
And it's full of dirty old dirt!

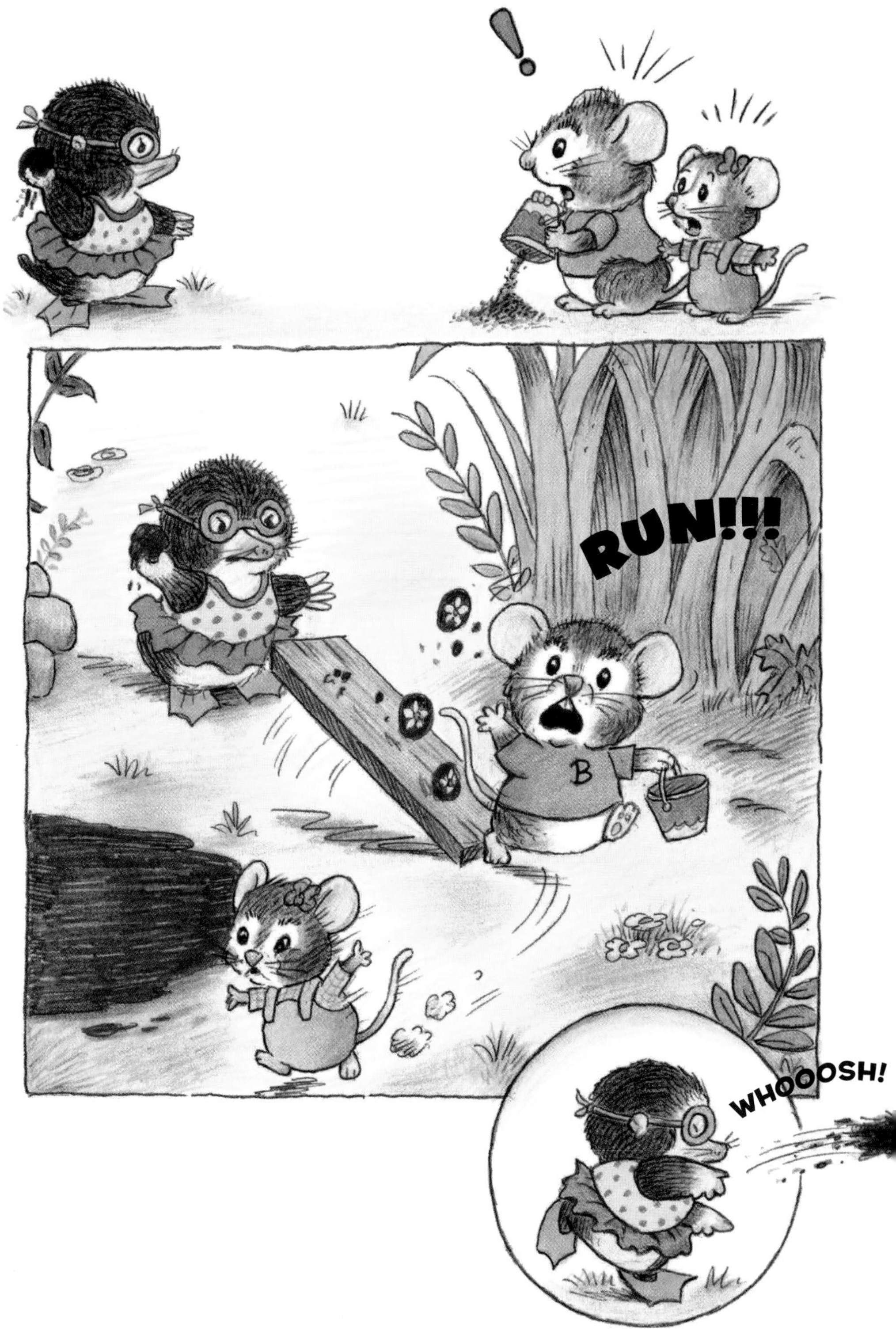
!
RUN!!!
WHOOOSH!

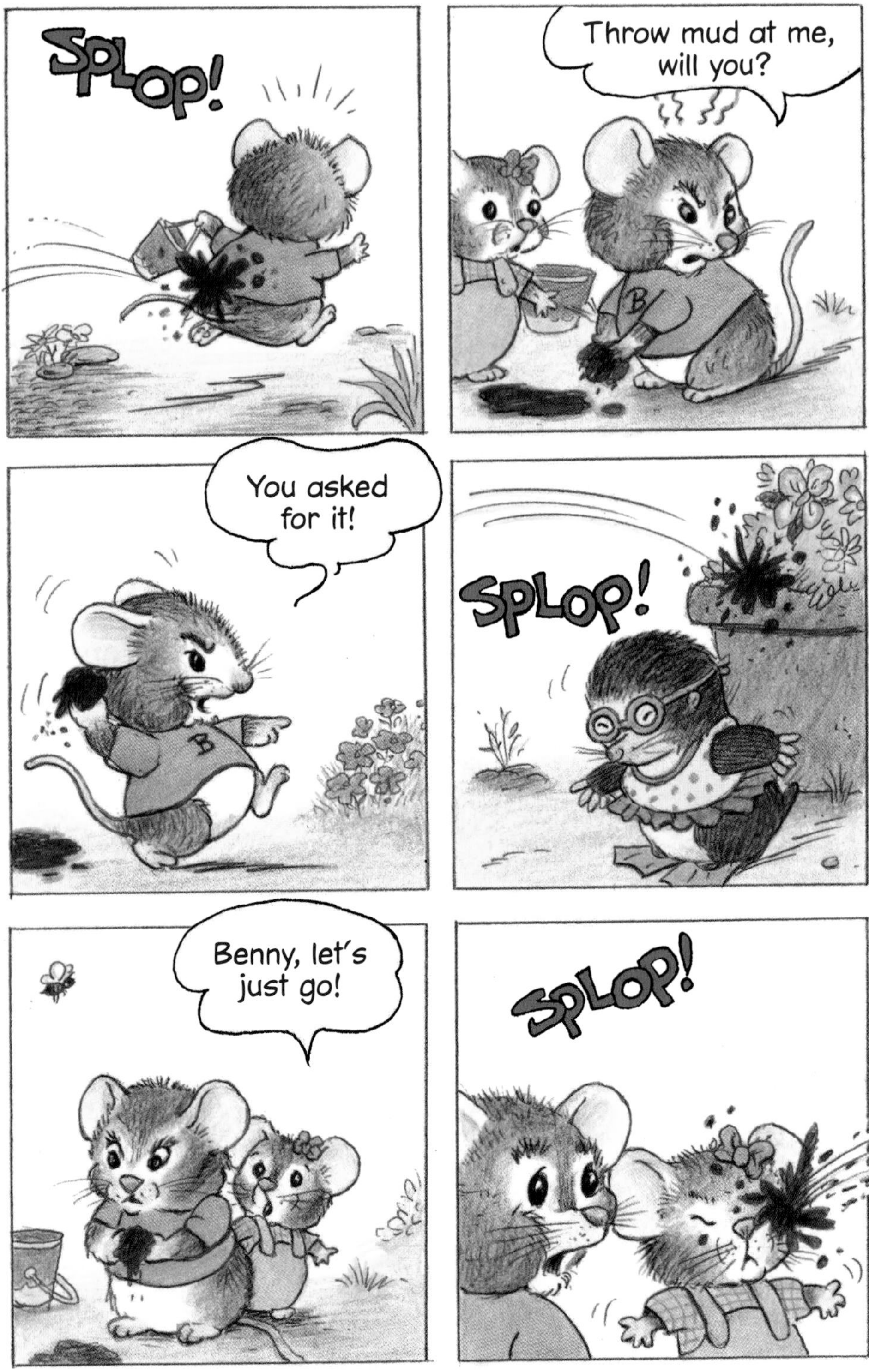
SPLOP!
Throw mud at me, will you?
You asked for it!
SPLOP!
Benny, let's just go!
SPLOP!

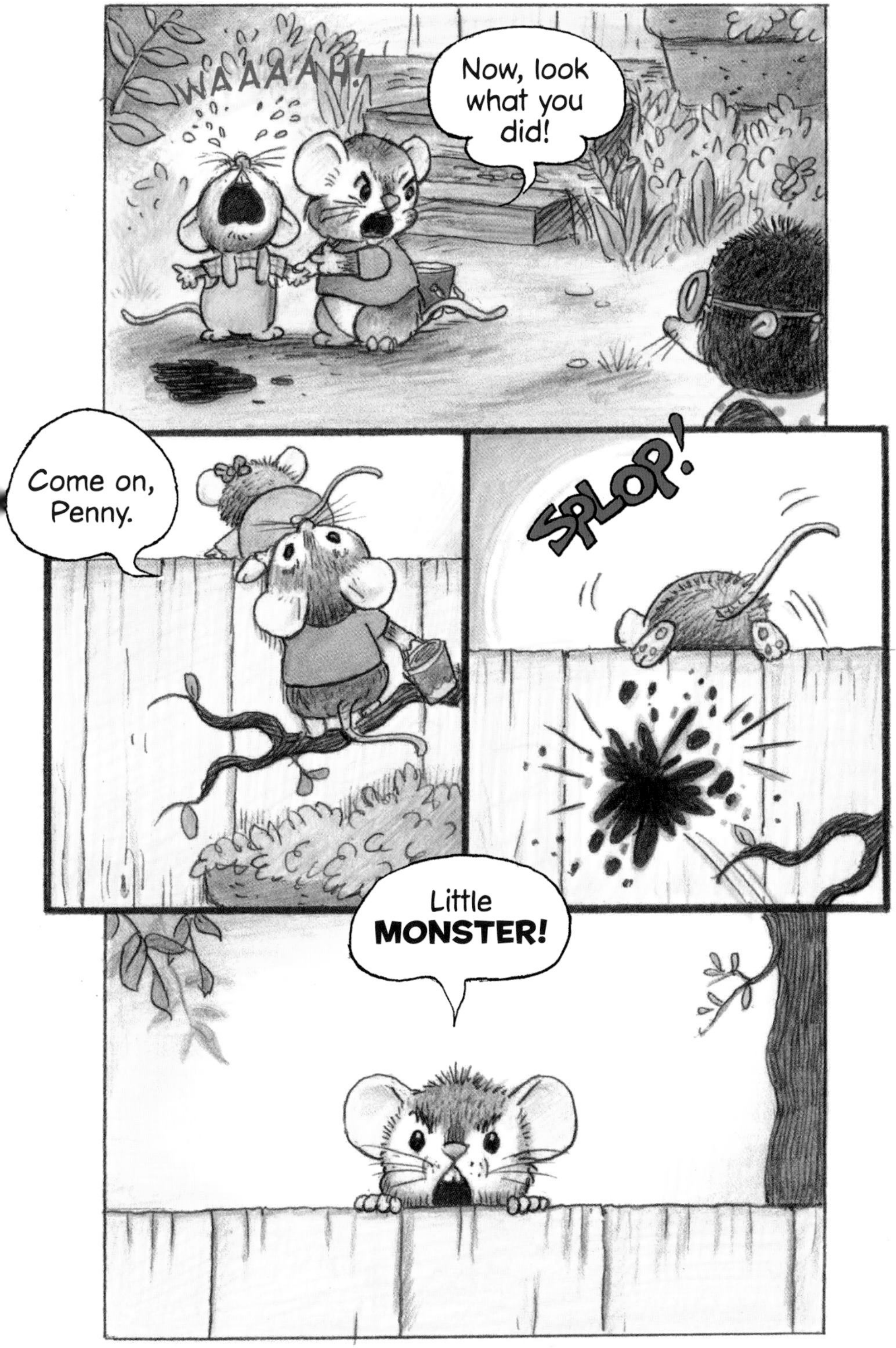
WAAAAH!
Now, look what you did!
Come on, Penny.
SPLOP!
Little MONSTER!

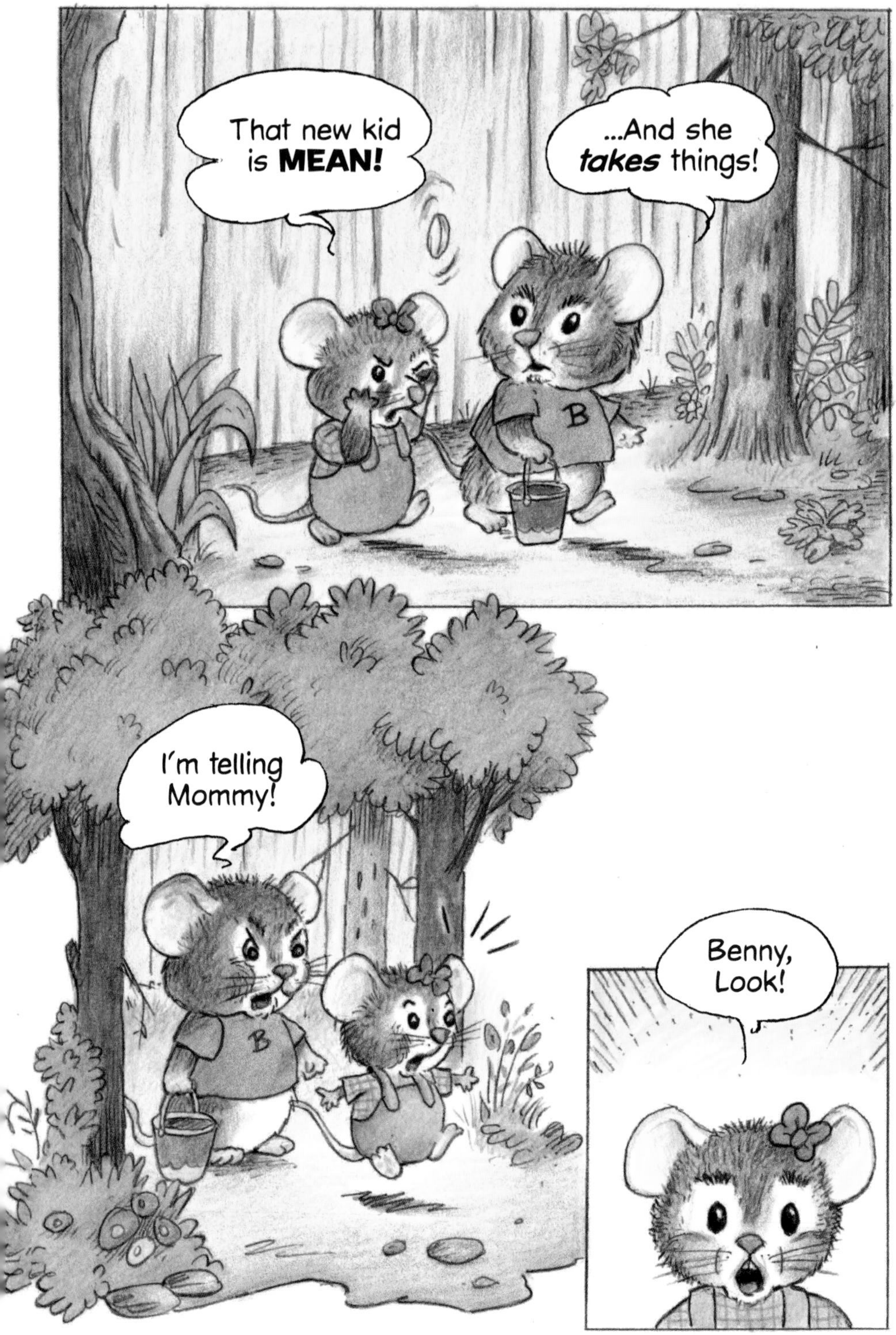
That new kid is **MEAN!**
...And she *takes* things!
I'm telling Mommy!
Benny, Look!

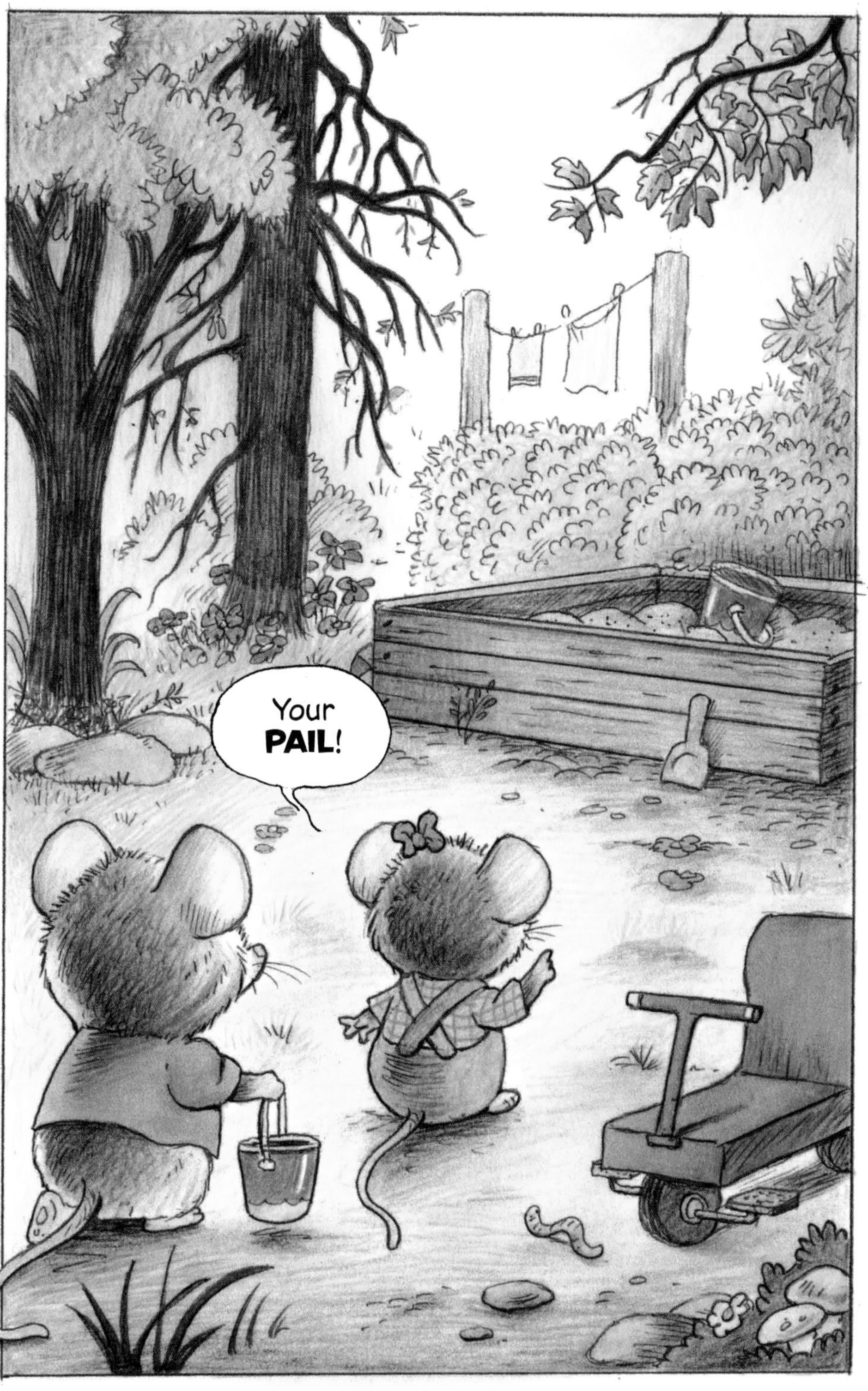
Your **PAIL**!

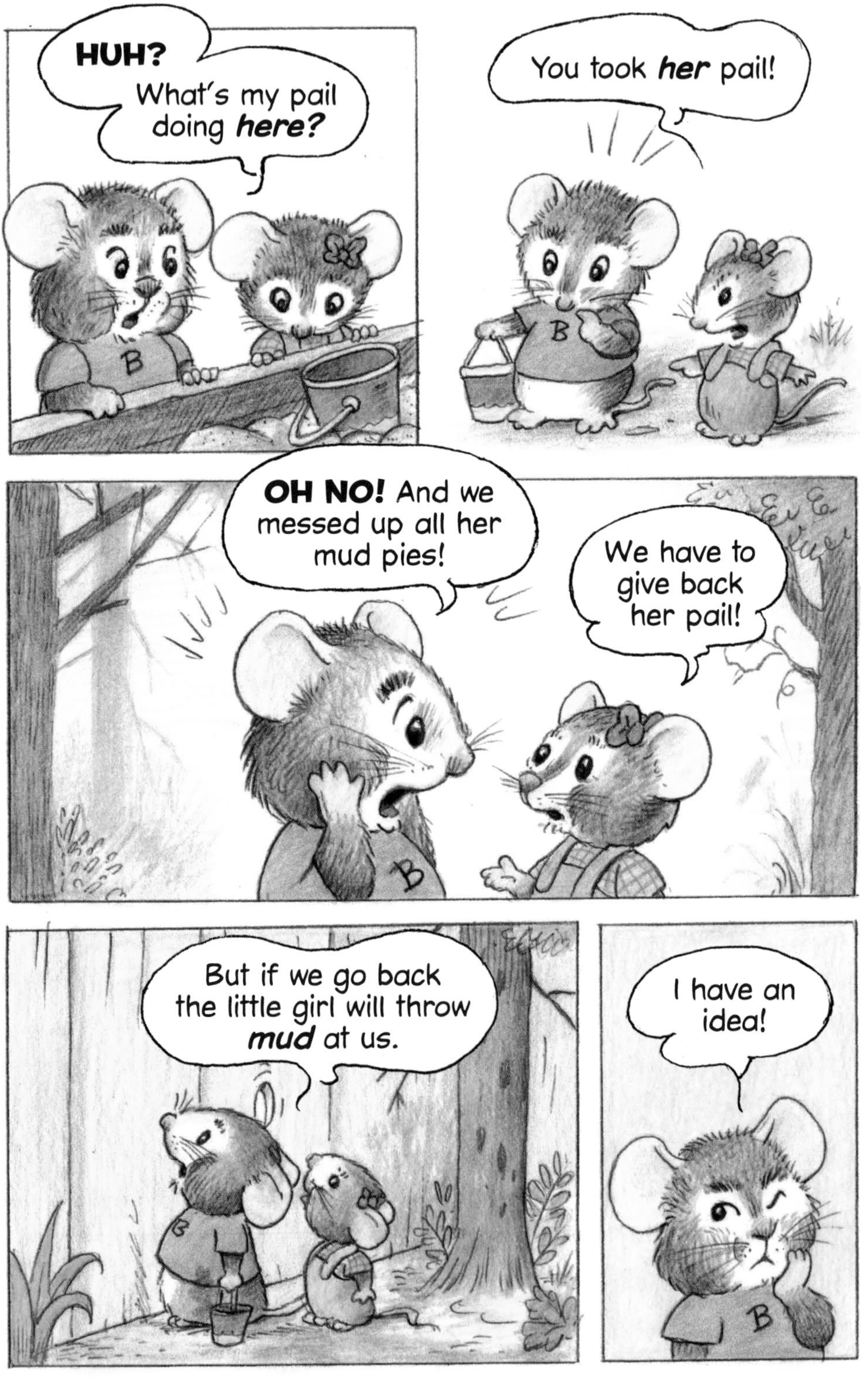
HUH?
What's my pail doing ***here?***
You took ***her*** pail!
OH NO! And we messed up all her mud pies!
We have to give back her pail!
But if we go back the little girl will throw ***mud*** at us.
I have an idea!

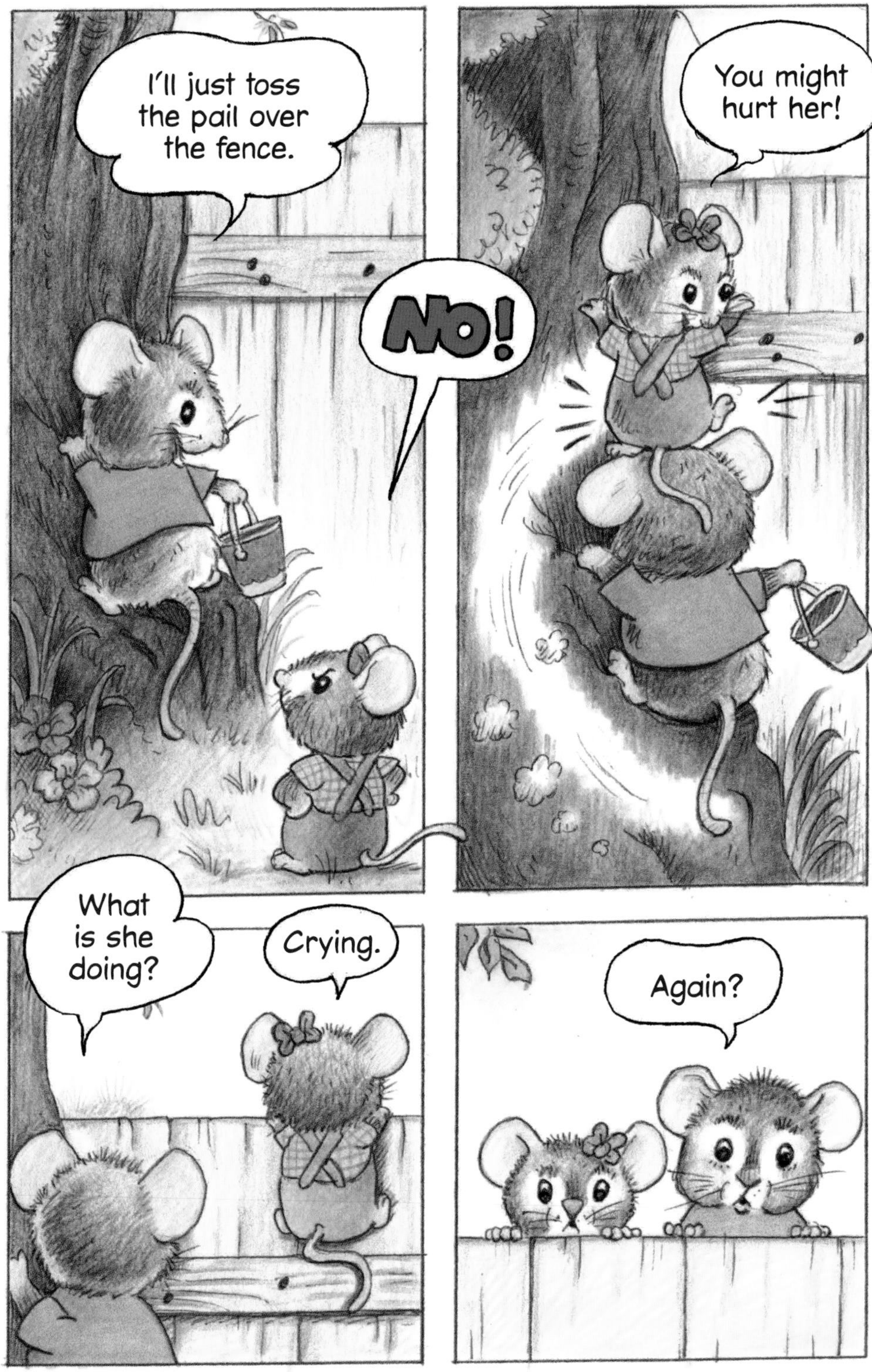
I'll just toss the pail over the fence.
NO!
You might hurt her!
What is she doing?
Crying.
Again?

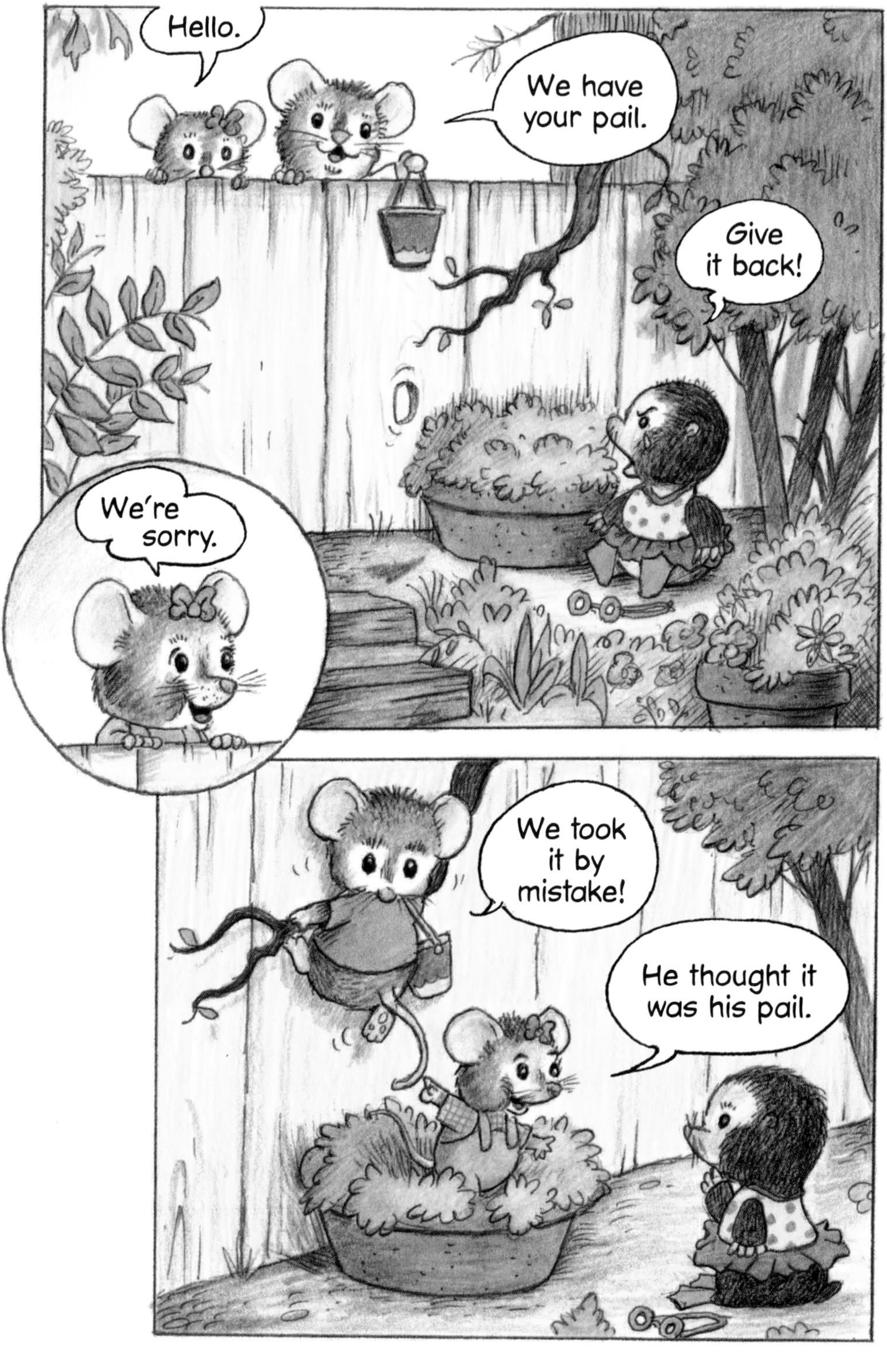
Hello.
We have your pail.
Give it back!
We're sorry.
We took it by mistake!
He thought it was his pail.

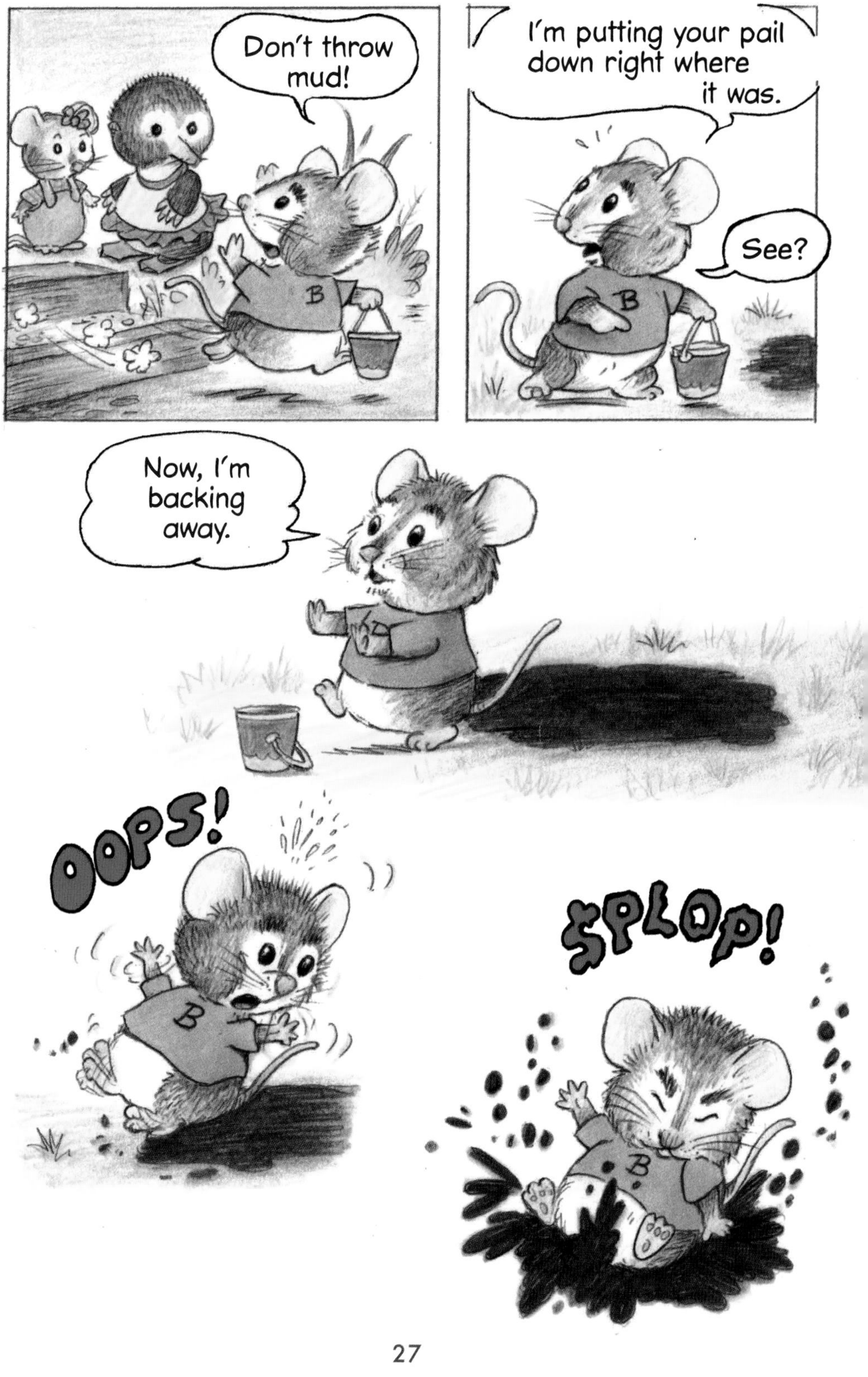
Don't throw mud!
I'm putting your pail down right where it was.
See?
Now, I'm backing away.
OOPS!
SPLOP!

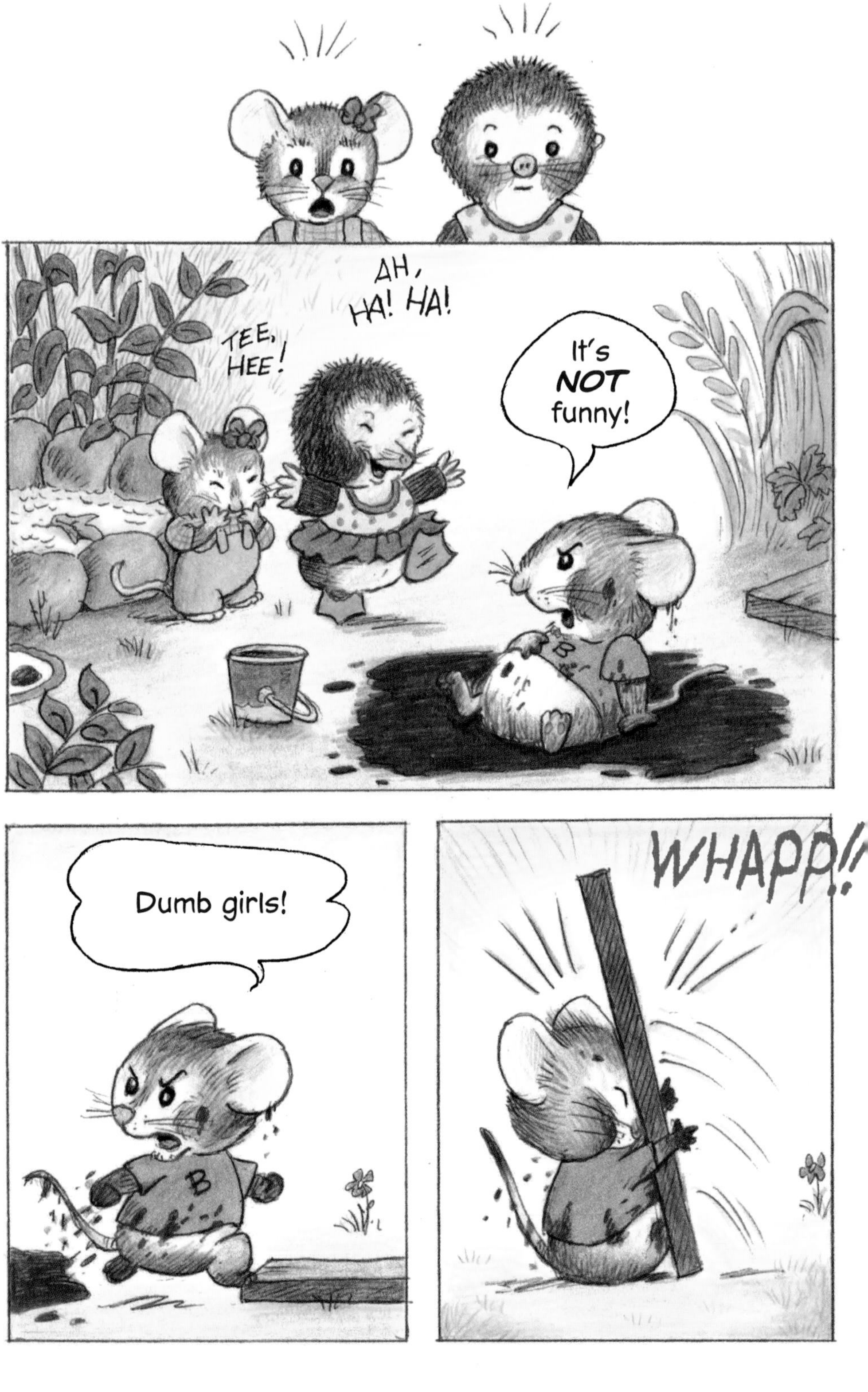
AH, HA! HA!
TEE, HEE!
It's **NOT** funny!
Dumb girls!
WHAPP!!

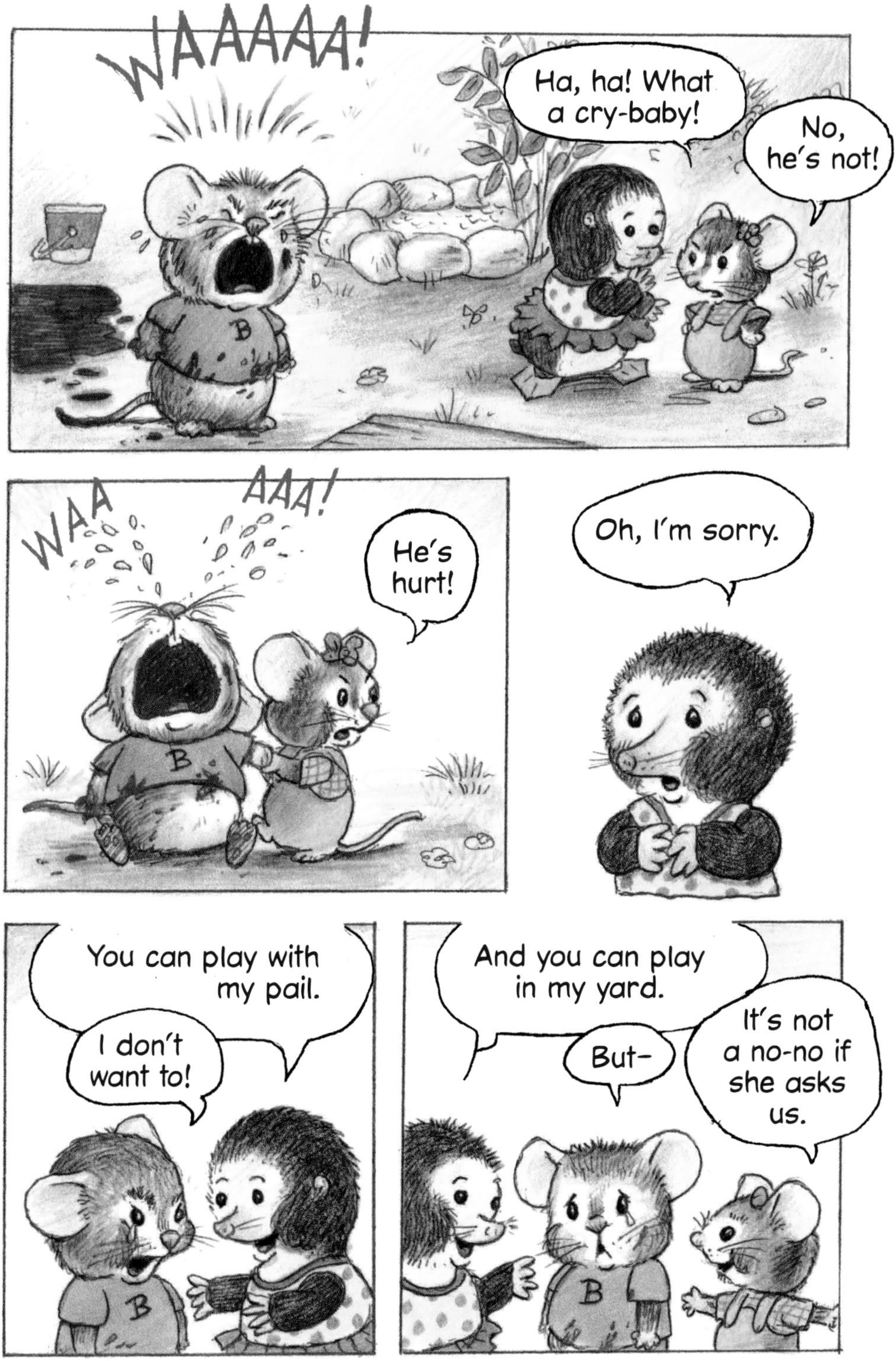
WAAAAAA!
Ha, ha! What a cry-baby!
No, he's not!
WAA AAA!
He's hurt!
Oh, I'm sorry.
You can play with my pail.
I don't want to!
And you can play in my yard.
But–
It's not a no-no if she asks us.

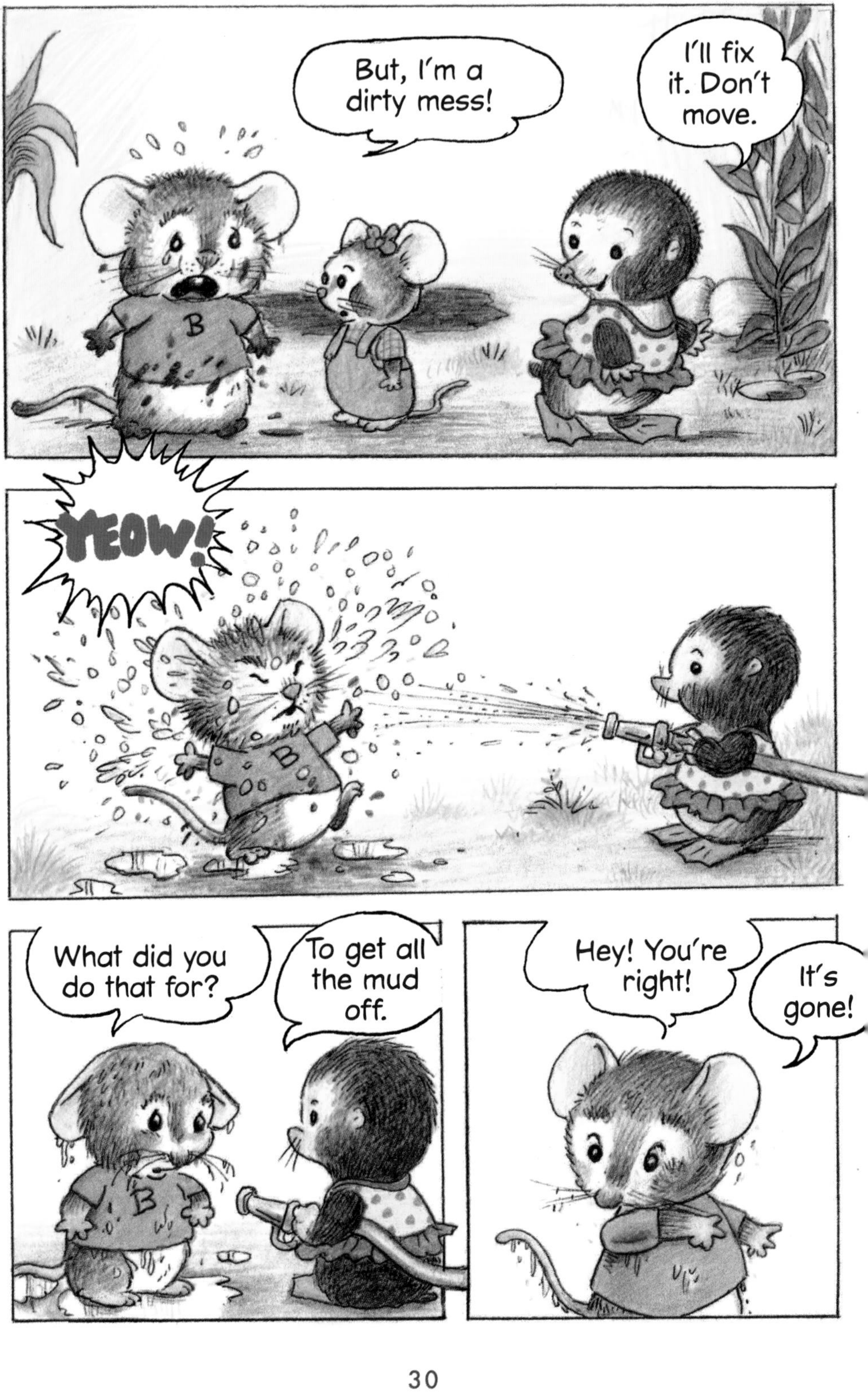
But, I'm a dirty mess!
I'll fix it. Don't move.
YEOW!
What did you do that for?
To get all the mud off.
Hey! You're right!
It's gone!

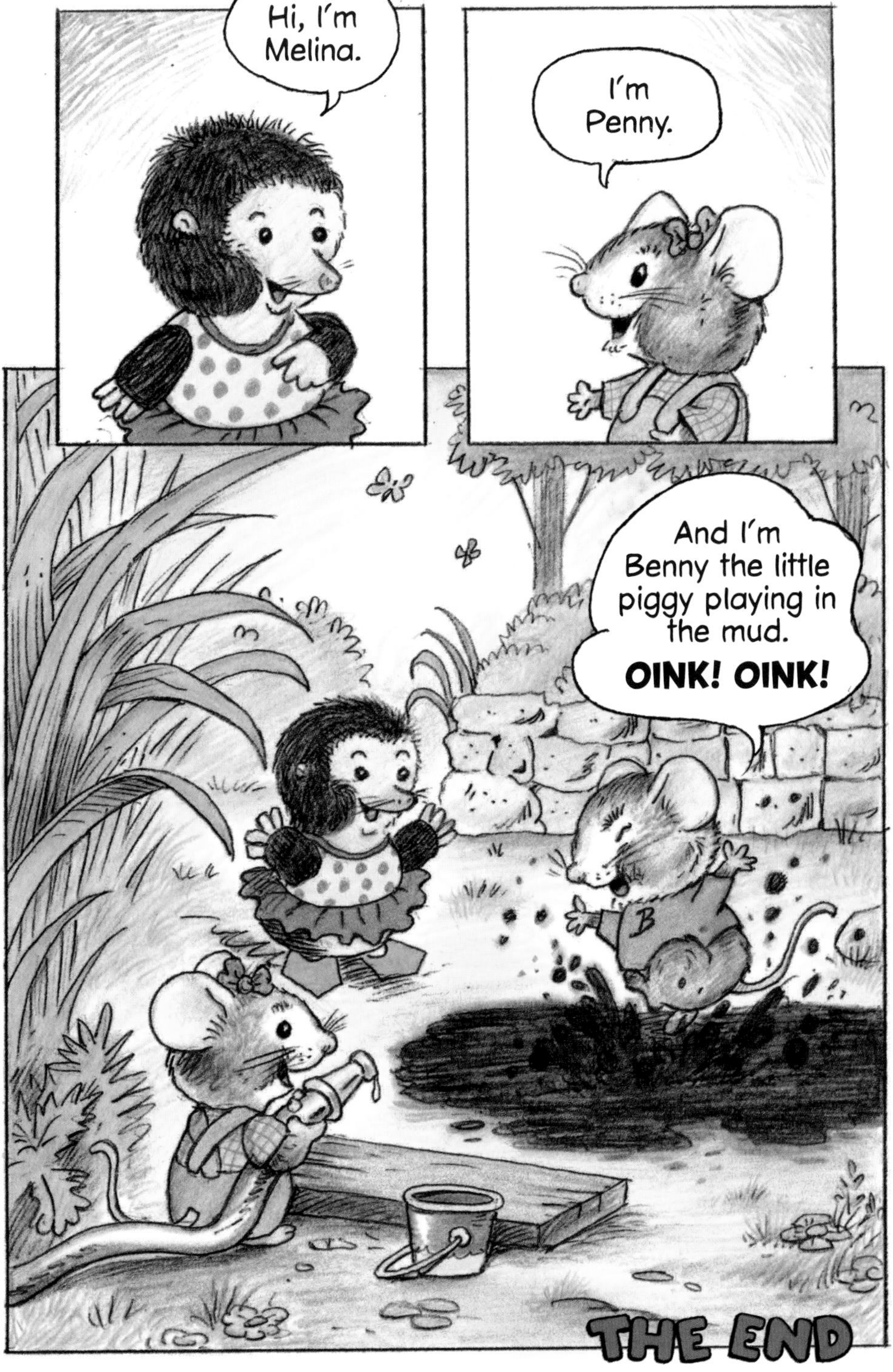
Hi, I'm Melina.
I'm Penny.
And I'm Benny the little piggy playing in the mud.
OINK! OINK!
THE END

ABOUT THE AUTHOR

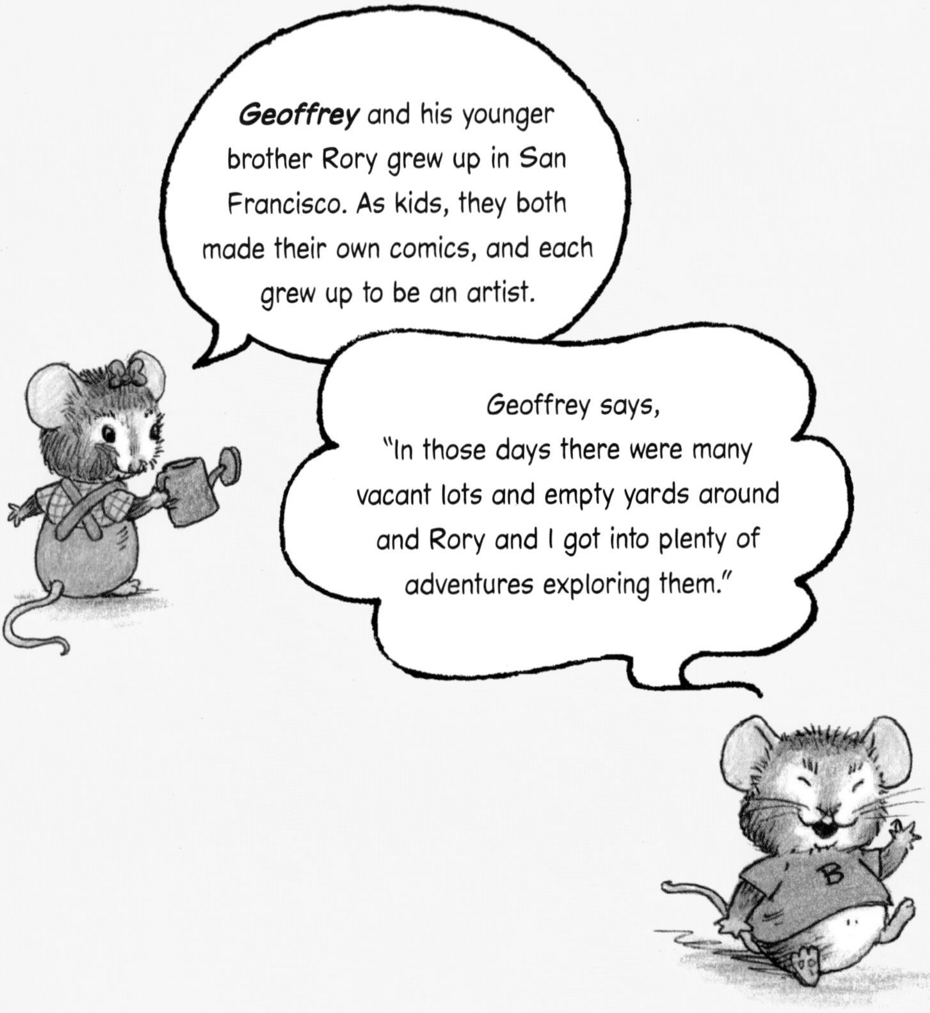
Geoffrey and his younger brother Rory grew up in San Francisco. As kids, they both made their own comics, and each grew up to be an artist.
Geoffrey says, "In those days there were many vacant lots and empty yards around and Rory and I got into plenty of adventures exploring them."
B

Geoffrey has written and illustrated over forty children's books, including the extremely popular series of early readers *Otto and Uncle Tooth*, the classic *Bear by Himself*, the *Patrick Bear* books, and *When the Wind Blew* by Caldecott Medal-winning author Margaret Wise Brown. His last TOON Book, *Benny and Penny in Just Pretend*, was praised in a *Booklist* starred review as "a charmer that will invite repeated readings."

TOON INTO FUN at TOON-BOOKS.COM

TOON READERS are a revolutionary, free online tool that allows all readers to **TOON INTO READING!**

TOON READERS: you will love hearing the authors read their books when you click the balloons. TOON READERS are also offered in Spanish, French, Russian, Chinese and other languages, a breakthrough for all readers including English Language Learners.

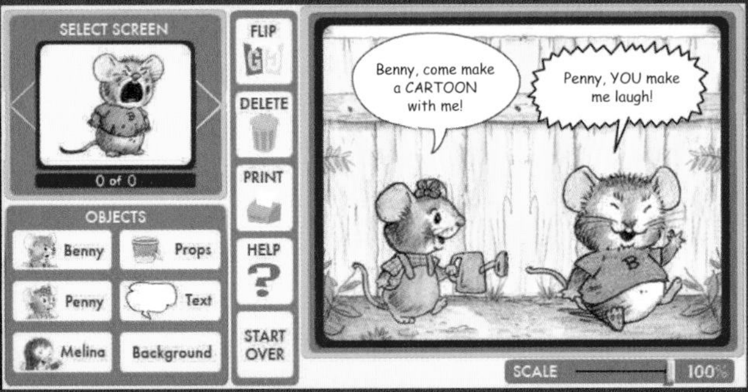

SELECT SCREEN
0 of 0
OBJECTS
Benny
Props
Penny
Text
Melina
Background
FLIP
DELETE
PRINT
HELP
START OVER
Benny, come make a CARTOON with me!
Penny, YOU make me laugh!
SCALE
100%

Young readers are young writers: our **CARTOON MAKER** lets you create your own cartoons with your favorite TOON characters.

Tune into our **KIDS' CARTOON GALLERY**: We post the funniest cartoons online for everyone to see. Send us your own and come read your friends' cartoons!

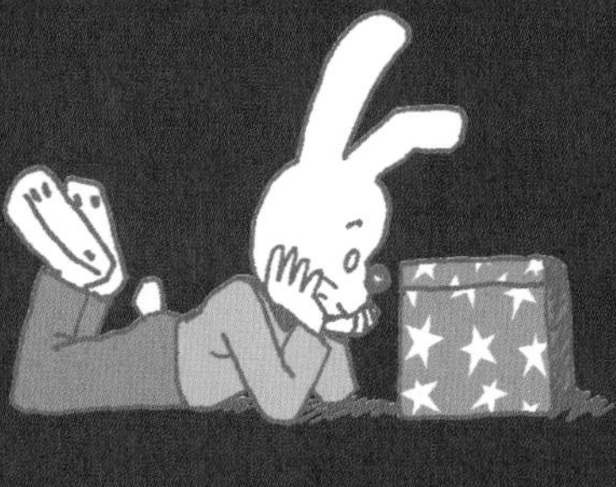

TOON into Reading

LEVEL 1
GRADES K–1
LEXILE BR–100 • GUIDED READING A–G • READING RECOVERY 7–10

FIRST COMICS FOR BRAND-NEW READERS

- 200–300 easy sight words
- short sentences
- often one character
- single time frame or theme
- 1–2 panels per page

LEVEL 2
GRADES 1–2
LEXILE BR–170 • GUIDED READING G–J • READING RECOVERY 11–17

EASY-TO-READ COMICS FOR EMERGING READERS

- 300–600 words
- short sentences and repetition
- story arc with few characters in a small world
- 1–4 panels per page

LEVEL 3
GRADES 2–3
LEXILE 150–300 • GUIDED READING J–N • READING RECOVERY 17–19

CHAPTER-BOOK COMICS FOR ADVANCED BEGINNERS

- 800–1000+ words in long sentences
- broad world as well as shifts in time and place
- long story divided in chapters
- reader needs to make connections and speculate

COLLECT THEM ALL!

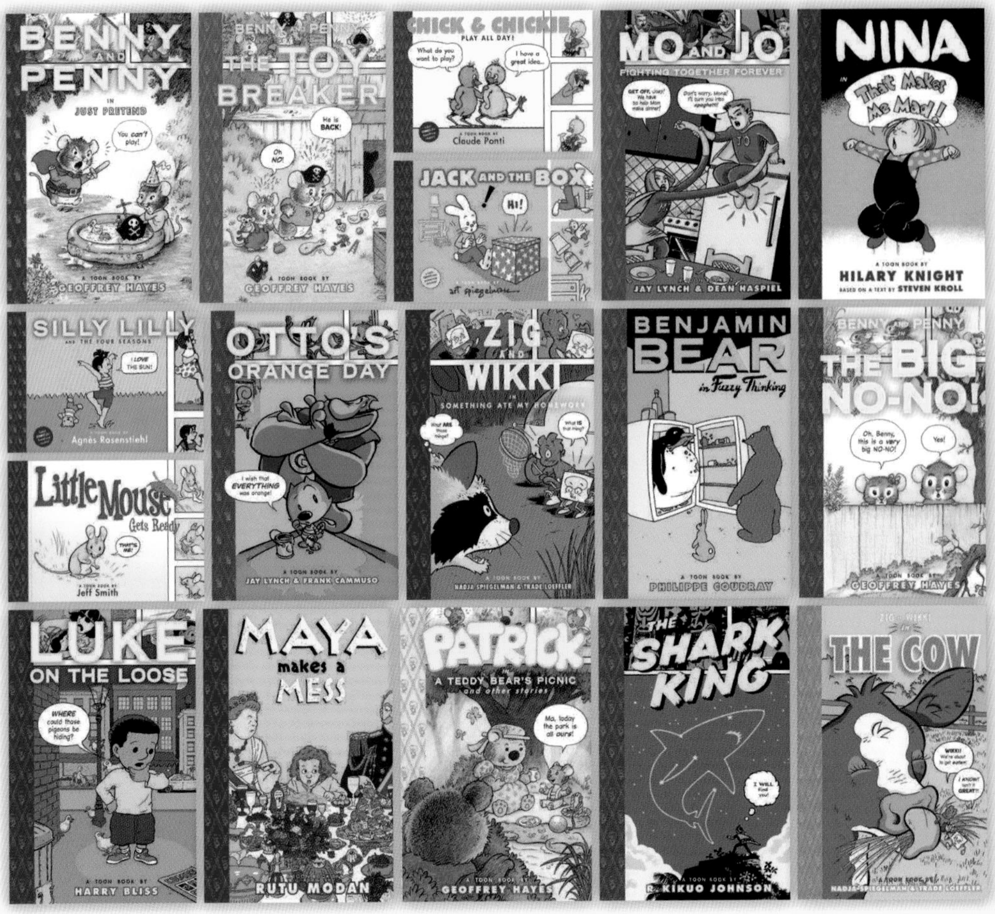
BENNY AND PENNY IN JUST PRETEND
You can't play!
A TOON BOOK BY GEOFFREY HAYES
BENNY AND PENNY THE TOY BREAKER
He is BACK!
Oh NO!
A TOON BOOK BY GEOFFREY HAYES
CHICK & CHICKIE PLAY ALL DAY!
What do you want to play?
I have a great idea...
A TOON BOOK BY Claude Ponti
JACK AND THE BOX
HI!
MO AND JO FIGHTING TOGETHER FOREVER
JAY LYNCH & DEAN HASPIEL
NINA IN That Makes Me Mad!
A TOON BOOK BY HILARY KNIGHT
BASED ON A TEXT BY STEVEN KROLL
SILLY LILLY AND THE FOUR SEASONS
I LOVE THE SUN!
Agnès Rosenstiehl
Little Mouse Gets Ready
A TOON BOOK BY Jeff Smith
OTTO'S ORANGE DAY
I wish that EVERYTHING was orange!
A TOON BOOK BY JAY LYNCH & FRANK CAMMUSO
ZIG AND WIKKI IN SOMETHING ATE MY HOMEWORK
A TOON BOOK BY NADJA SPIEGELMAN & TRADE LOEFFLER
BENJAMIN BEAR in Fuzzy Thinking
A TOON BOOK BY PHILIPPE COUDRAY
BENNY AND PENNY THE BIG NO-NO!
Oh, Benny, this is a very big NO-NO!
Yes!
A TOON BOOK BY GEOFFREY HAYES
LUKE ON THE LOOSE
WHERE could those pigeons be hiding?
A TOON BOOK BY HARRY BLISS
MAYA makes a MESS
RUTU MODAN
PATRICK IN A TEDDY BEAR'S PICNIC and other stories
Ma, today the park is all ours!
A TOON BOOK BY GEOFFREY HAYES
THE SHARK KING
I WILL find you!
A TOON BOOK BY R. KIKUO JOHNSON
ZIG AND WIKKI IN THE COW
NADJA SPIEGELMAN & TRADE LOEFFLER

TOON BOOKS SET 1

Set of 10 hardcover books	978-1-61479-298-7
Benny and Penny in Just Pretend	978-1-61479-148-5
Benny and Penny in the Toy Breaker	978-1-61479-149-2
Chick & Chickie Play All Day!	978-1-61479-150-8
Jack and the Box	978-1-61479-151-5
Mo and Jo Fighting Together Forever	978-1-61479-152-2
Nina in That Makes Me Mad!	978-1-61479-153-9
Otto's Orange Day	978-1-61479-154-6
Silly Lilly and the Four Seasons	978-1-61479-155-3
Silly Lilly in What Will I Be Today?	978-1-61479-156-0
Zig and Wikki in Something Ate My Homework	978-1-61479-157-7

TOON BOOKS SET 2

Set of 8 hardcover books	978-1-61479-298-7
Benjamin Bear in Fuzzy Thinking	978-1-61479-299-4
Benny and Penny in the Big No-No!	978-1-61479-300-7
Little Mouse Gets Ready	978-1-61479-301-4
Luke on the Loose	978-1-61479-302-1
Maya Makes a Mess	978-1-61479-303-8
Patrick in a Teddy Bear's Picnic and Other Stories	978-1-61479-304-5
The Shark King	978-1-61479-305-2
Zig and Wikki in the Cow	978-1-61479-306-9